HOW TO SURVIVE TIME TRAVEL

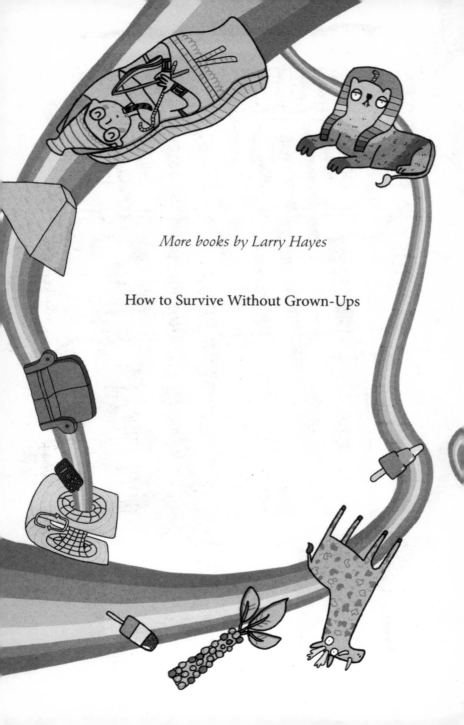

More books by Larry Hayes

How to Survive Without Grown-Ups

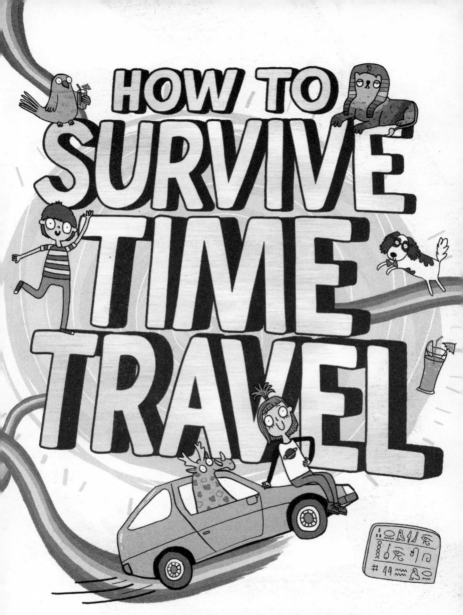

HOW TO SURVIVE TIME TRAVEL

LARRY HAYES

ILLUSTRATED BY KATIE ABEY

SIMON & SCHUSTER

First published in Great Britain in 2022 by Simon & Schuster UK Ltd

Text copyright © 2022 Mewrite Limited
Illustrations copyright © 2022 Katie Abey

1 3 5 7 9 10 8 6 4 2

Simon & Schuster UK Ltd
1st Floor, 222 Gray's Inn Road
London
WC1X 8HB

www.simonandschuster.co.uk
www.simonandschuster.com.au
www.simonandschuster.co.in

Simon & Schuster Australia, Sydney
Simon & Schuster India, New Delhi

A CIP catalogue record for this book is available
from the British Library.

PB ISBN 978-1-4711-9836-6
eBook ISBN 978-1-4711-9837-3
eAudio ISBN 978-1-3985-1151-4

This book is a work of fiction. Names, characters, places and incidents
are either the product of the author's imagination or are used
fictitiously. Any resemblance to actual people living or dead, events or
locales is entirely coincidental.

Printed and bound by CPI Group (UK) Ltd, Croydon, CR0 4YY

MIX
Paper from
responsible sources
FSC
www.fsc.org   FSC® C171272

For the real Eliza and Johnnie, who came up with most of the funny bits, and who are NOTHING LIKE the Eliza and Johnnie Lemon in this book. And for Sophie, who is special. And also for Iris – I promise that a character with your name is coming soon.

A LONG TIME AGO

It's a long time ago, 5000 BCE to be exact, and things are bad.

THAT'S ME, I'M THE HERO OF THIS STORY. I'M NOT PANICKING

You're probably wondering what I'm doing here. My name is Eliza and I'm falling off a sofa into a artificial volcano that's about to erupt 7,053 years ago and wipe the entire human race off the face of the Earth.

My baby brother, Johnnie, has it worse. He's choking on a sherbet lemon, and he's about to cough it right into the school bully's – Sadie Snickpick's – face.

Johnnie faces a triple threat:

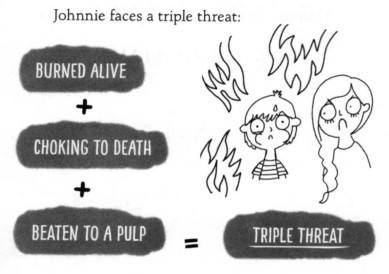

BURNED ALIVE

+

CHOKING TO DEATH

+

BEATEN TO A PULP

=

TRIPLE THREAT

You're probably worried about us. You're probably holding your breath, thinking, *Won't they be suffocated by the fumes long before they get burned alive?*

But don't panic – never panic, ever. It won't help. I learned this the hard way, a long time in the future.

THE YEAR 2053

(A LONG TIME IN THE FUTURE)
HOW NOT TO PANIC
(THE HARD WAY)

I used to worry all the time.

Then something happened in my life, and soon worrying wasn't an option any more. I had to learn *not* to worry.

You can read all about it in my old journal. My publishers have turned it into a 'Major Publishing Event', which is basically a book called *How to Survive Without Grown-Ups*.

It's got all the gory details in there – you should

read it. Or I can probably sum it up here and save you a *lot* of time . . .

A few weeks ago, my parents were abducted by Noah, a maniac billionaire with a massive eyeball. He computer-hacked their brains and sent them to Mars, and it was at that point that I realized there's no point worrying, because bad stuff will or won't happen, so you may as well get on with <u>your</u> life rather than **worrying** about whether your parents are going to be **Brainless Robots for ever.**

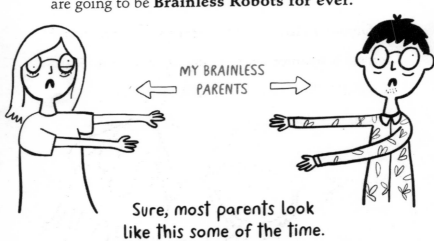

MY BRAINLESS PARENTS

Sure, most parents look like this some of the time. But this was my mum and dad all the time. Like they're staring at a phone. But without the phone.

Or **worrying** about whether the big eyeball guy

– Noah – was ever going to bring them back.

THIS IS NOAH

THIS IS THE BIG
EYE I WAS TELLING
YOU ABOUT

Yep, just Noah.
No surname or anything.
Always be suspicious of
people who only have one
name. Apart from Jesus
obvs. And God.

Or **worrying** about whether your annoyingly

genius baby brother is going to have his FACE

SUCKED AWAY BY A VAMPIRE SQUID.

JOHNNIE
WITHOUT
A FACE

Not so genius now,
eh, little brother?

OK, hold up. I can see this might all seem a bit **_deranged_** and a lot confusing. This is a whole new journal, and it looks like you're not gonna go and read my first one, so let me give you a **SUPER-QUICK, FOUR-PIC SUMMARY:**

MICROCHIP
INSERT

EMPTY SPACE WHERE
THE SPACE ARK USED
TO BE

Back on Earth, after surviving all *that*, I just stopped worrying.

It was great.

For almost a month, it was absolutely fantastico.

Well, not *completely* fantastico. Being a ten-year-old in the year 2053 is pretty horrendo (the toilet tells your parents if you're not eating enough fibre, sweets come with pictures of dead people on them, and school dinners are grown in a lab). And, besides, none of my old problems ever really went away.

My PE teacher was still trying to kill me.

MR MURRAY IS TRYING TO KILL ME

MASSIVE AND HARD

And Mrs Crosse, my maths teacher, was still totally evil.

She's the first teacher in the history of world teaching to give a kid a nickname and not the other way round.

And it was worse because it was true: I still didn't have any friends.

BUT that's not *my* fault. The school bully, Sadie Snickpick, has had it in for me since Reception. She just hates me. And, if anyone else talks to me, Sadie stuffs their head down the toilet. Making friends is kind of hard when you're up against that.

Thankfully, I had Myrt. I know, it's tragic – ten years old and my BFF's a dog – but it's better than nothing (even if Myrt's really angry most of the time and a bit bitey[1]).

---

1 One really important thing you need to know about Myrt is that she *hates* anything orange. She just goes wild. All because of a puppyhood incident, which I don't like to talk about because it was kind of my fault.

OK, if you really want to know . . . When I was a toddler, I fell on top of Myrt when she was watching that old movie *Finding Nemo* and her brain now thinks that anything orange is about to attack her. So she attacks first.

THIS IS MYRT BTW

She looks sooo cute.
Even when she's
biting you.

But, anyway, I didn't *just* have Myrt; I also had my **family**. I know it sounds puke-level corny, but my family really were the best thing about my life: Mum, Dad and Johnnie. They were great. Weird as a fish beard, but great.

MEET THE WEIRDO FAMILY

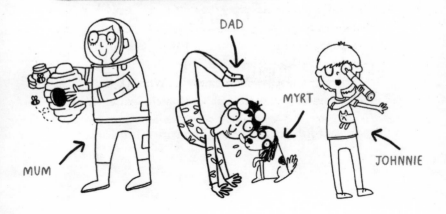

MUM

DAD

MYRT

JOHNNIE

OK, Johnnie was still a bit of a pain. I love him to bits, but that doesn't stop him being a five-year-old genius who just sucks attention like a giant attention-sucking black hole.

Basically, my mum ate loads of sardine sandwiches when she was pregnant and this happened:

PARENTS GLASSY-EYED IN AWE

PLAYING MOZART ON A PIANO HE'S BUILT WITH LEGO

I JUST WANTED MY CHEERIOS

But even if Johnnie can be a bit annoying sometimes

Mum and Dad are genuinely great.

I mean, Dad's totally distracted half the time, but when he isn't he's super fun. I think I told you that Noah computer-hacked Dad's brain – he put a microchip in it and turned him into a robot. Well, what I didn't tell you was that, after we rescued Dad, he decided to *keep the microchip in*, because: 'Think of all the possibilities!'

He's permanently linked to the internet now, so he can do 'Jedi stuff'.

DAD'S JEDI STUFF

THAT TENSE LOOK
ON HIS FACE?

Is Dad trying to
flush with mind
power?

SMART TOILET

Mum took the microchip out of *her* brain. Which was a mixed blessing to be honest. Mum's amazing. She can make a garden feel like paradise; she makes our home feel like the best place in the universe. But she can be a bit *clingy*.

She's just a bit full-on. She likes to get involved and solve everything. Like, *everything*. You can't even have a tiny little rant about a teacher without her immediately phoning the school office. But we'd come to an understanding. I just had to say, '**BACK OFF, MUM**,' and she'd back away, frightened, like I'd turned into an instant teenager.

So things were OK – not just survivable but genuinely OK. And, besides, we'd just broken up from school for the summer holidays. And they were going to be the best summer holidays ever, because we had a book deal that was going to make us even richer than the Snickpicks, and we also had access to our own secret (and slightly creepy) tropical island that had really cool stuff on it, like robot apes and giant turtles you could ride on.[2]

But then, all of a sudden, things were NOT OK.

It all started when my parents disappeared.

And I don't mean they 'left home' (like they did the last time) or they 'went missing'. I mean they literally disappeared. Literally. They just vanished right in front of my eyeballs.

We were all in the garden on one of those long summer afternoons when it feels like nothing bad can ever happen ever again. Johnnie was building something out of Lego that could actually fly. I was teaching Myrt to bring us eggs in her mouth without crushing them, and my parents were fiddling about with a car we'd stolen from Noah.

---

2 You still haven't read Book 1? I can't explain everything; I'm telling you, stop reading this NOW. Book 1 is blow-your-mind brilliant.

I say *we'd* stolen it, but in actual fact it had been dumped in space after Noah had been kind of vaporized by a bomb, so I don't think it was technically a crime. More like tidying up litter.

So, anyway, about this car. One minute my mum was shouting at my dad because he'd passed her the wrong spanner:

The next minute the whole thing had disappeared: car, Mum, Dad, spanner, everything.

All gone.

In their place was a really old little oak tree. The kind that fairies would use (if they existed). It was mostly eaten away by time and by woodlice and by lightning and it had stumpy little branches, like arms. It was the sort of tree you'd feel clever for hiding in during a game of hide-and-seek, but wish you hadn't once you were inside because it's full of bugs that climb down your neck and start trying to live in you.

Anyway, the tree was really, really old and totally new at the same time. I should know: I've lived in that house for ten years and there's never been a tree there before.

'Well, I guess they got the time machine working, then,' said Johnnie. 'I'd better get the chainsaw.' And, with no further explanation than that, off he went to get Dad's chainsaw from the shed.

Now, you probably noticed the words 'time machine' in that sentence, but at that moment I was more focused on the word 'chainsaw'.

Johnnie's a genius, but he can also be really dumb.

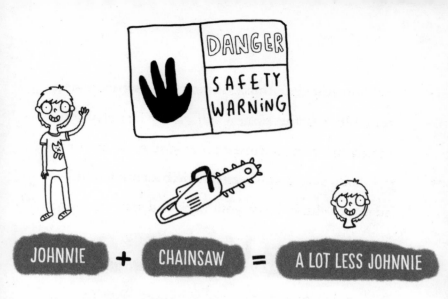

JOHNNIE + CHAINSAW = A LOT LESS JOHNNIE

And there's not much of Johnnie to start with.

'You can't use that, you idiot. It's too heavy. You'll fall over and land on it, and chop your leg off. Your good one.'

Johnnie has a weak left leg. It stops him running and walking down stairs. So the thought of losing his good leg made him hesitate.

I snatched the chainsaw out of his hands and he toppled backwards with the change of weight. You'd think that would prove my point, but Johnnie just did his red-cheek thing. Which means he's gonna have a meltdown.

'Eliza, we've got to see how old it is.'

I looked at the tree. It really did look like a little old man.

LITTLE OLD TREE **VS** LITTLE OLD MAN

'It's a million years old. So what? Don't you get it? Mum and Dad have just *vanished*. Into thin air!'

Johnnie rolled his eyes. 'Obviously.'[3]

---

3 He knows I hate it when he says that. He learned it from our big cousin Olive. Try it next time you want to annoy someone – it totally works. It's like you're calling them 'pointless and stupid' every time you say it.

'So where'd they go?'

'Wrong question,' answered Johnnie. 'You mean *when* did they go?'

'About two minutes ago. Obviously.'[4]

'Not when did they *leave* – when did they go *to*? When did they *arrive*?'

I looked blank, and had to force my mouth shut. Because it was only then that the words 'time machine' hit my brain. And they hit it like a sledgehammer.

'You do know the car's a time machine?' said Johnnie.

I didn't know that. My parents never tell me anything. But I wasn't going to admit that in front of my baby brother, so I just said nothing.

---

4 I was really pleased to get an 'obviously' in, but he didn't seem to notice, which is typical Johnnie.

Johnnie poked at some bark on the new-old tree. 'Can't you even see it?'

I looked, and there was something. Kind of a word scratched into the tree.

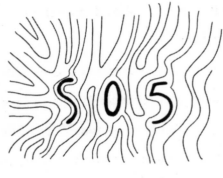

'So five?'

'No, ess-oh-ess obviously,' said Johnnie irritably. 'Someone over shoulder? That just doesn't make sense.'

'As in Save Our Souls. Obviously.'

That's when I had my first-ever panic attack.

It started with pins and needles in my face, then my hands and feet went numb, then the rest of me. I just had time to think, *Why do Mum and Dad always have to ruin everything?* when the vision in both my eyes went completely grey and I fell over. Right on top of the chainsaw.[5]

I came to, choking on a sherbet lemon. Johnnie's stubby little finger was ramming it into the back of my throat.

'Are you trying kill me???' I asked, shoving him away and coughing it out.

'It's a sherbet lemon.' He picked it off the grass and offered it back to me. 'Sherbet lemons make everything better, especially panic attacks. The sugar gives your brain extra energy and the lemon makes your mouth produce spit.'

I stared at him, my mouth filling with spit.

'Your brain calms down because the spit tricks it into thinking it's about to eat a nice meal and so . . .' He trailed off lamely.

'So you almost choked me to death?'

'Eliza, don't you understand? Mum and Dad are

_____

5 Don't worry – it wasn't on or anything.

trapped. They're stuck somewhere in the past, and this is their way of letting us know when to rescue them.'

I took the sweet, but it was covered in grass.

'So you're saying Mum and Dad sent us this tree as a message?'

Johnnie nodded and I looked back at the tree.

'It's not much of a message, is it?'

'Of course *that's* not the message. The message is *inside.*'

Sometimes Johnnie can be a bit cryptic. And it's always annoying.

I looked at him, and waited.

'We need to cut down the tree and count the rings. To find out when it was planted.'

I looked at the tree. It seemed about 10, 000 years

old. The thought of Mum and Dad stuck in the Stone Age made my brain fizz.

'Johnnie, this is a total and absolute disaster!'

Johnnie nodded.

But then Sadie Snickpick turned up.

Which *was* a total and absolute disaster.

HOW TO STAND UP
TO A BULLY

My first reaction was to have another panic attack: tingling in cheeks, numb feet. Sadie Snickpick's droopy smile began to look blurry and grey, and I had one terrible thought:

What if I pass out and wee myself? In front of Sadie Snickpick, the world's biggest bully?

She probably had her phone. And she'd definitely take a photo.

No one could survive that. It was the worst thing that could ever happen to anyone.

Ever.

We'd have to move.

To a different planet.

Then I remembered that 'we' was just me and
Johnnie ∧ now Mum and Dad were GONE. My head
started spinning again. This time I really was going
to pass out.

But the gods smiled on me that day. Or maybe I
should thank Johnnie – I still had the sherbet lemon.
The grassy, spitty, sticky one.

It was in my hand. And I got it into my mouth
and sucked.

TOP 3 WORST THINGS THAT
COULD EVER HAPPEN TO
ANYONE, EVER

#3   Call the teacher Mummy

#2   Spill milk on yourself and
       smell like cheese all afternoon

#1   Have a panic attack, faint and
       wee yourself while Snickpick's
       around with a camera

I sucked hard and my mouth filled with spit. And almost immediately I felt better. The grey blur lifted and I focused on Sadie Snickpick's teeth. Her smile was a sneer.

'Rescue *who* with a chainsaw?'

She'd been listening all right, but for how long? How much had she heard?

'What are you doing here?' I swallowed some lemon-flavoured spit.

She handed me a School Fundraiser leaflet and kept staring at me.

'Rescue *who* with a chainsaw?' she repeated, her voice even sneerier. She inched forward, like a gorilla ready for a fight.

I didn't know what to say. There was no answer. No answer that wouldn't lead to a world

told ya!!!!

JohNNie xx

of pain. She'd tell her parents, the school, the world. Thoughts tumbled around my brain. We'd be sent to an orphanage. Or, worse, we'd have to live with Gran.

I sucked my sherbet lemon. It was the only thing standing between me and total disaster. You see, Sadie Snickpick is the worst kind of bully.

Sadie Snickpick is a **Level 3** Bully.

SCHOOL BULLY LEVELS

Level 1 Bully:
The Bonehead

Level 2 Bully:
The Snevil

Brutal

Sneaky AND evil

Level 3 Bully:
Sadie Snickpick

Brain like a chess computer
(She's always ten moves ahead).

Actual biceps
(She even had them in Reception)

Weirdly big hands
(But really small feet! What's that about?)

Brutal AND sneaky AND evil

Everyone always says that bullies are cowards.

'You just need to stand up to them,' they say. 'If they give you a nickname, give them one back; if they punch you on the arm, punch them in the face.'

I know, for a fact, that doesn't work.

Some bullies aren't cowards – they're really brave and tough and clever. And they can literally punch your teeth out.

I was thinking all this through when Johnnie's voice came to the rescue.

'We're rescuing a squirrel that's stuck up a tree.'

I looked at Johnnie and he smiled back, a bit too pleased with himself.

MY FIRST
SCHOOL PHOTO

Sadie Snickpick snorted in disbelief.

'Squirrels don't get stuck in trees. They *live* in trees, you moron.'

And then Johnnie made the biggest mistake in the history of mistakes.[6] It was a mistake so bad that it was going to completely destroy our lives, and maybe worse.

'It's just a game,' he said, blissfully unaware that his life would never be the same again. 'It's just a game, **_dumb-head_**.'

I flinched and shut my eyes. He'd just called Sadie a **_dumb-head_** and I couldn't bear to see what would happen next.

You think I was overreacting?

Then it's high time you learned a little bit about Sadie Snickpick.

---

6   You may have noticed I'm really into Top 3 lists at the moment.

TOP 3 BIGGEST MISTAKES IN THE HISTORY OF THE PLANET

#3   Eating an apple (in the Garden of Eden)

#2   Inventing cabbage

#1   Calling Sadie Snickpick a dumb-head

When we were still in reception, a boy once called Sadie Snickpick 'stupid'.

Nikolas Porter was in Year 5. He was cool, good at football and everyone liked him. Sadie Snickpick kicked his ball out of the playground so they couldn't play football where she wanted to play something else.

He'd called her 'stupid' because she'd done it on purpose. He was right to call her stupid – what she did was stupid. *And, besides*, he thought, *she's only a reception kid. Right?*
Wrong.

Her revenge was fast and brutal. The ball incident was Monday lunchtime. By Friday he'd been kicked out of school. For ever.

WE NEVER SAW NIKOLAS PORTER AGAIN.

NIKOLAS PORTER
POPULARITY: 92
HEIGHT: 4'10"
AGE: 10
Evil Viciousness: 12

SADIE SNICKPICK
POPULARITY: 11
HEIGHT: 3'7"
AGE: 4
Evil Viciousness: 100

You think I'm exaggerating? You think no Reception kid could possibly be evil-vicious enough to get a Year 5 kid thrown out of school for ever?

Then think on.

Actually, read on:

Do you get it now?

Do you understand??

Johnnie was doomed.

He might be a genius, but against the raw, animal-savage Sadie Snickpick, he didn't stand a chance. Sadie Snickpick knows no rules. Nothing is beyond her. Even the teachers are afraid of her. Even head teachers.[7] Even other kids' parents.

And Johnnie had just called this nuclear missile a **dumb-head.**

Sadie Snickpick looked him up and down. 'You're Johnnie, aren't you?'

Johnnie nodded. He was still smiling.

'When do you start school, Johnnie?'

I shut my eyes again.

'In September,' said Johnnie proudly but starting to sound less sure of himself.

---

7 It's true – I once saw Mrs Valentine giggle like a little girl when Sadie told her to extend break time.

'No one will play with you, Johnnie. Not even your sister.'

I opened my eyes. Johnnie's cheeks were bright red.

'OK, but you're still a dumb-head.'

I couldn't believe it. He just didn't know when to stop. For a genius, he's such an idiot.

It was Sadie Snickpick's turn to go red. She flushed right up into her hair. I thought she was going to shout, or scream, or launch herself at Johnnie's throat. I saw the muscles in her fingers start to twitch and for a moment I thought Johnnie was literally dead meat.

And then a car honked its horn. A long, angry blast that shook Sadie out of her herself. For a second, she almost looked afraid, and I realized it must be her mum or dad getting impatient. But Sadie's sneer was back in a heartbeat.

'Don't worry, little man,' she said, looking down her pointy nose at Johnnie. 'I'm going to enjoy destroying you.'

Then she stepped forward and flicked him. Right on his left eyeball. So fast Johnnie didn't even have time to blink.

He collapsed with a howl and started screaming. Even I was shocked.

Then she looked at me, with her Don't-You-Dare Stare. 'If I see you help him, I'll destroy you too,' she said quietly.

I just stood there, rigid with dread, and she laughed.

The car honked again, even more angrily. Sadie flinched again. But then she laughed and turned, disappearing round the front of the house. Seconds later a massive car sped away from our house, kicking up dust and stones.

It was only when the car disappeared from view that I bent down to cuddle my sobbing little brother.

'Thank you,' he said, pressing his face into my chest.

And I can say in total honesty that I've never felt more ashamed in all my life.

'You're a hero, Johnnie, standing up to Sadie like that.'

'Or an idiot,' he said, looking at me with one eye.

I just nodded.

HOW TO SURVIVE
WITHOUT PARENTS

When your parents disappear, there's no one to make things better. There's not even anyone to make lunch.

On the other hand, there's no one to stop you from having ice cream for lunch.

Once Johnnie had stopped crying, and we'd made sure he wasn't blind in one eye, we sat down with some triple-fudge-choc-chip.

'We can't stay with the cousins,' said Johnnie. 'They're allergic to dogs.'

'And they live in Australia, Johnst.'

Johnnie sucked some melted ice cream through his straw while he thought about that.

'Whatever happens, we can't let Gran know,' I said with my mouth full.

Gran's idea of childcare is to look disappointed all the time. She isn't happy unless I'm looking ashamed about something. On top of that, she thinks Myrt's the devil. Just because Myrt bites her now and again.[8] If we went to live with Gran, Myrt would end up in a cage, or worse – in a dogs' home for bitey dogs.

Johnnie shook his head.

'We've got to tell someone. We can't do this on our own, Eliza.'

'Johnnie, we just have to wait it out. That means we can't let *anyone* know – school, cousins, friends. Anyone.'

But Johnnie shook his head again. 'No way; Mum

---

8   It's all totally Gran's fault for wearing that horrible old orange cardigan.

and Dad are stuck. We need to go get them, and we can't do that on our own.'

'Except they've got the time machine, haven't they?' Usually Johnnie was smarter than this. 'Don't worry, little brother, they'll figure out how to get back. We just need to survive the summer holidays. It'll be easy, I promise.'

The latest edition of Johnnie's *The Book of Secrets* had a whole chapter on 'How to Have the Best Summer Holiday Ever' and I intended to use it.

If you don't have a copy of *The Book of Secrets*, get one. **It will change your life**.

Trust me, there's a chapter on every possible thing you will ever want to know: How to Hypnotize your Parents, How to Get M&Ms for Breakfast, How to Win Sports Day (when you're rubbish at running), How to get Jedi Mind Powers . . . *everything*.

But Johnnie was still shaking his head and there were tears in his eyes again.

'You don't understand, 'Liza. If they were coming back, then they'd be back by now.'

'What do you mean?' I said. 'It's only been half an hour.'

But I suddenly knew exactly what he meant.

Mum and Dad had a time machine. If they'd ever got it working *at any time in the past*, then they'd be back already. It's not like they'd come back in a year's time or even a week's time. They'd be back right now, full of smiles and hugs and amazing stories.

'Mum and Dad are gone for ever,' said Johnnie, his face red and determined. 'If we ever want to see them again, we've got to go and get them. And for that we need help.'

'No! Whatever we do, we do it alone. You can't trust people, Johnnie. You should know that by now.'

'What do you mean?' Johnnie looked really worried.

'You'll understand when you get to school,' I said. 'People are only interested in themselves. Trust people and you get hurt.'

'But Dad always says . . . stuff.'

Johnnie was floundering. I was definitely winning the argument.

'What sort of stuff?'

'I dunno . . . stuff like: "Alone we're just a drip, together we're an ocean." He says we have to trust people, or life's impossible.'

'Life *is* impossible, Johnnie. You'll learn that when you get to school.'

'But—'

'No buts, Johnnie. Dad always says, "Don't trust anything you see; even salt looks like sugar . . ."'

'And poo looks like mud,' finished Johnnie.

'So,' I said firmly, 'we can't trust anyone. Whatever we do, we do it alone.'

But what *should* we do?

That was the real question.

As I sat there on the lawn, looking at Johnnie's wibbly face, with Myrt's warm head flopped on my lap, I realized this was one of those moments.

One of those moments in life when everything is about to change. Moments like that don't happen often, and when they do you hardly ever know it at the time. But this time I somehow knew it. I knew that what I said next would probably be the most important sentence I'd ever say. Ever.

I looked at Johnnie. His little face looked ready to crumple. So what would it be?

'Let's just wait it out.'

Or . . .

'OK, let's risk everything and go rescue Mum and Dad.'

I knew, even then, that travelling back in time

would be a horrendo, but even *my* imagination didn't guess quite how crushingly awful it would be. I'd rather swim through a sea of vampire squid than do it again. And, if I'd known what was to come, I'd have curled up under a blanket with Myrt and cried myself to sleep.

But I didn't. That's the thing, you see. If we knew what was coming next in life, we'd probably just stay in bed. But we don't. So we're optimistic about things. And, besides, the thought of never seeing Mum and Dad ever again left me feeling sick. We couldn't just sit and wait.

I didn't even know if we'd be able to build our own time machine, so I just said, 'OK, Johnster, we can chop the tree down anytime. First up, we need to build a time machine.'

HOW TO BUILD A
TIME MACHINE

Time machines get invented all the time.

In movies . . .

You've seen it all before. Building a time machine involves loads of electricity and great special effects. There's probably some cool music thrown in too. A mad professor comes out of a barn, looking crazy-eyed. A bit of lightning later and, whoop-whoop, off you go. Probably to the wrong date.

But if it were that easy humans would have done it ages ago. Mainly because whenever people time travel in movies they get worshipped as **gods**, which must be pretty cool.

Building a time machine, it turns out, is a lot more complicated than you'd think. Luckily for us, Noah had already figured everything out. And he'd left diagrams and a working time machine in the shape of the car. Mum and Dad might have disappeared with all of that, but Dad always wrote everything down in his journal. It's the one thing we've got in common.

Dad's journal was the key.

He kept it next to the thinking hammock in his workshop. It was the place we used to hide when Mum was cross with us.[9]

It was weird going into Dad's workshop without him. It was an old tobacco barn and it smelled of all-things Dad. Engine oil, wood shavings and cheese sandwiches, mainly. It was even weirder reading his journal. I could hear Dad's voice in my head as I looked down the page headings.

I suddenly felt shaky. Maybe I'd never hear his voice for real ever again. Would I one day forget what it sounded like? But there wasn't time for thoughts like that, so I squashed them down and read quickly.

There was so much crazy Dad-invention stuff to

---

9   Dad has a firm rule that no one in the thinking hammock can be disturbed. Ever. Even if the shed is on fire. According to Dad, ideas are too important.

skip past, but I finally found it.

'How to Build a Time Machine,' I whispered to Johnnie, and he smiled, all eager-faced.

The first page was complicated, but reassuring. Time travel happens all the time, apparently.

Facts about time travel

Fact 1. Time travel happens a lot, but only for really small things like single atoms. Wormholes pop into existence all the time – atoms get sucked down them and end up somewhere and somewhen else in the universe.

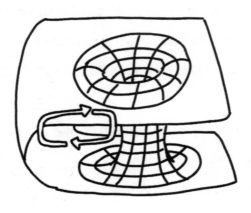

Then the wormhole disappears.

I turned to Johnnie.

'So, we need a wormhole,' I said unconvincingly.

Johnnie snatched the diary, and I shouted a protest, but my heart wasn't in it. Building tech stuff was Johnnie's thing.

He flicked through page after page, his little face going pinker and pinker.

'It's all here already,' he said excitedly, jumping down. He shoved the journal at me and ran over to Dad's workbench. There was something covered in a sheet. Johnnie pulled it off.

'Look, there's the atom-scanner.' Johnnie pointed excitedly. 'It scans something right down to atom level. Look at Dad's picture.'

I glanced down at the journal on my lap and, sure enough, there was something identical drawn out in precise black ink.

This went on and on, with Johnnie dragging dust sheets off anything he could reach.

'It's all here, Eliza. We just have to put it together and we're good to go.'

'Sit down, baby brother. I want you to write down on one sheet of paper *exactly* how to build a time machine. No fancy words. Just write it down in English.'

Johnnie took a big breath.

'It's probably easier if I give you the simple version first.' Then he drew this:

HOW TO BUILD A TIME MACHINE (simple version)

Sending Gran's rock cakes back to the Stone Age (where they belong)

Gran's rock cake is too big.

STEP 1:

Turn Gran's rock cake into a RECIPE for Gran's rock cake.

STEP 2:

Shrink the recipe so it's smaller than an atom.

STEP 4:

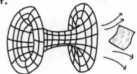

Send the mini-recipe to the past.

'OK,' I said slowly. 'So you don't send the rock cake back; you send a tiny little recipe for the rock cake back.'

Johnnie nodded.

'But what about Step Three? You've missed out Step Three.'

'Oh yeah, that's the complicated bit. You also have to send the recipe for a machine that can remake it when it gets there.'

'What, like an oven?'

'Yeah,' said Johnnie slowly. 'Something like that – a *recipe* for an oven.'

Now *that* just didn't make any sense.

'*A recipe for an oven?* Then how does the oven get made? In the past, I mean? Don't you need a machine to *make* the oven? And then you'd need *another* machine to make *that* machine?'

My head was spinning.

'That's the genius bit. The oven just kind of makes itself.'

'Kind of?'

'Well, think about when you started off. You were just a little egg cell that kept doubling and doubling until it made a baby Eliza.'

How to make a baby Eliza

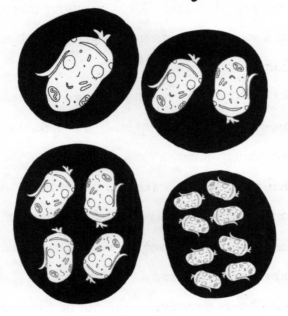

'It's just like that. Except it starts off even smaller.'

'Smaller than an atom?'

'Yep, really small.'

'So the recipe for Mum and Dad and the car and the machine to remake them is all smaller than an atom?'

'Yep, and it all got sucked down a wormhole. Cool, huh?'

I looked at Johnnie carefully, and then back at all the stuff in the workshop.

'OK, baby brother,' I said, walking back out into the sunlight. 'You put it together; I'll make lunch. Just don't muck about.'

I shut the door to make my point, but it was then that I realized we weren't in any hurry at all. Johnnie could take as long as he wanted to build his time machine. We had a whole summer holiday to enjoy. Endless sunny days without parents to tell us what to do: when to go to bed, when to brush our teeth, when to stop eating sugar, when enough movies is enough.

Johnnie could take as long as he liked – Mum and Dad were stuck in the past. So the only thing that mattered was when we went back *to*, not when we went back *from*. We could have one summer holiday, and then go back in time, rescue Mum and Dad, and then we could come back from back in time to the *beginning* of the summer holidays!

Yes, we were gonna have **TWO SUMMER HOLIDAYS**.

Johnnie isn't the only genius in the family.

I went into the kitchen, got some pizza out of the freezer and put the oven on. *This afternoon*, I thought to myself, *I'm going to watch a 12A rated film, even though I'm only ten.*

I put my feet up and watched an old Harry Potter movie with Myrt sitting on my lap. 'This summer holiday,' I told her, 'is going to be the best two ever.'

HOW TO HAVE THE BEST TWO SUMMER HOLIDAYS EVER

Parents think that all kids want, all the time, is all-out action. Hour after hour of theme parks, scuba-diving, kite-surfing, water parks, exotic food, indoor skydiving, climbing walls, walks in the park, Shakespeare in the Park, bungee jumping. What a nightmare!

Don't get me wrong – some kids might live for that kind of stuff, but most of the time us kids just want to be left alone. Time out from being told what to do by grown-ups. My number-one parenting tip is: **'LEAVE US ALONE!'**

If you just did that, the world would be a much better place.

In fact, a whole summer with me in charge sounded like the best thing ever. And now was my chance to prove it.

The first morning was a bit tricky, but we soon got the hang of it. We added a ton of ice cream to the supermarket order and no one seemed to complain. And, after a day without being fed, Myrt started cleaning our plates and the kitchen floor just like *The Book of Secrets* said she would.

Mum's weekly video call with Gran was a **worry**, but once we found some old videos of Mum saying: 'You're probably right,' we just stuck it on a loop and things went fine.

In fact, we got the hang of it surprisingly quickly . . .

With Johnnie busy working on the time machine, you'd think I'd get lonely, but after a few hours of lockdown I realized I was made for this. With Myrt in tow and the sun out, I had the best summer ever. Yeah, sure, I was worried about Mum and Dad. But I just had this feeling that it was all going to be OK. Johnnie would put the time machine together, we'd go and get them, and everything would be *just* fine.

But no paradise can last for ever. There's always a snake lurking somewhere. And our paradise was no exception. It was doomed from the beginning. Doomy-doom-doom doomed.

Sadie Snickpick was the snake in our paradise. And one morning, in the middle of Week Two of the Best Summer Holiday Ever, the snake turned up on its new bike: her mouth dripping venom.

Our paradise was gone in sixty seconds.

HOW TO SURVIVE A SNAKE BITE

Have I mentioned that Sadie Snickpick is evil?

You probably still think she's just a bit of a Mean Girl. An End-of-Level Baddy. But she's not. She's not even The Final Boss. She's way beyond that; she's **PURE EVIL**.

If you still don't believe me, then watch this:

She reached out and handed me an **envelope of doom**. I opened it with a shaking hand. Whatever was inside was going to be awful, I just knew. My mind spiralled wildly out of control, but even my imagination didn't realize quite how bad it was going to be.

'I've invited the whole school.' The braces on her

ELIZA LEMON

INVITES **YOU** TO AN END-OF-HOLIDAY

Fancy Dress
Garden-Skydiving Party
BRING ALL YOUR FRIENDS
(Because I've Got None)

Sunday, August 4th, noon till late.
RSVP: Or don't.
Wibbly Cottage, Lower Biscuit.

smile glinted like cobra fangs. 'I'd like to see *you* organize a fancy dress, garden-skydiving party for two hundred kids in two days without any parents to help.'

Sadie looked genuinely happy for the first time in her life.

'One way or another, you're going to have to tell the truth, *orphan girl*!'

My mouth was dry and my throat felt like a grizzly bear had sat on my voice box. And, besides, there was nothing I could say to make things right. This was game over, and we both knew it.

In forty-eight hours the world would know we had no parents.

Sadie Snickpick bunny-hopped her bike round and rode off in a cloud of dust.

We were doomed.

Suddenly my mind turned to Johnnie, sweating

away in Dad's workshop all by himself, trying to put together a time machine against impossible odds while I watched movies and played with Myrt. And then I realized: even *Myrt* was in Dad's shed helping out. I felt awful.

'Johnnie!' I shouted, and he came running out, with Myrt round his ankles.

'What?' he answered, lifting up his welding goggles.

'We're running out of time. We need to cut down the tree.' I laid my hand on the rough old trunk.

'But I thought you said—'

'That was before. We're almost out of time.'

'Can I do it?' he squeaked, with a sudden smile, and Myrt barked.

'No, Johnst,' I said quietly, taking off Mum's turban, and wiping away some of my eye make-up.

'Bring the chainsaw. I'll do it.'

HOW TO KILL A TREE

It was time to open up the tree.

I'd grown to quite like it. The mossy trunk was super soft, and the perfect shape for kicking back and reading a book in the shade. I'd never known my grandads, but the little-old-man-tree made me wonder about them. Stupid, I know. But chopping it down felt like murder.

At the very least, it was a crime against nature. And if we've learned anything over the past fifty years it's that nature will come back and bite you on the butt if you mess with it too much.

All of this seemed to pass right over Johnnie's head. For a second time, he dragged Dad's chainsaw out of the shed. This time I didn't even speak. He handed me the safety visor, and then the chainsaw itself. The battery light flashed green and it rumbled into life at the flick of a switch.

It wasn't as heavy as Johnnie made it look and, before I could think too much, I lifted it to waist height and felt the chainsaw bite into the ancient wood. I cut through thousands of years, through winters and summers and storms and snow. I cut right deep into its core. To the little sapling in the middle that had grown from an acorn.

The chainsaw screamed as I sliced and cried. And then, with a sudden, heavy lurch, the trunk began to crack and groan. The whole thing ripped apart, and I jumped sideways as the tree came crashing towards me. Do NOT try this at home.

It missed me, but smacked into the conservatory, bending iron and smashing glass with so much noise that my heart bounced. I turned to check on Johnnie.

He was standing to one side with the biggest grin you've ever seen.

'There's something inside.' He struggled up on to the stump and started pulling at something lodged in the wood.

It came free with a big heave and Johnnie fell backwards, clutching a crusty old piece of leather.

'Is that a dead animal?' I asked.

'No. I think it's a shoe,' he said. 'Look.'

I snatched it off Johnnie and turned it over in my hands. It did look like a dead animal, but he was right – it was a shoe. Dad's shoe.

That made *no* sense. Why would Dad send us a shoe?

'So what is it?' I said. I felt angry, but I didn't know why.

'It must be some kind of a message from Dad. A *clue*,' said Johnnie. 'We just have to solve it.'

HOW TO SOLVE A SHOE

Solving a shoe, it turns out, is easy. There was writing on the tongue in biro.

God knows why he'd used a shoe. Maybe he didn't have any paper. Johnnie thinks it's because shoe leather lasts a long time. And that's just the sort of thing Dad would think of.

'Solve the Riddle of the Sphinx's Butt,' said Johnnie in a Scooby-Doo voice.

'I think it's just "Solve the Riddle of the Sphinx".'

Johnnie shrugged and I checked the co-ordinates on my phone. The little Sphinx picture didn't lie. It was smack-bang in the car park for the pyramids of Giza.

'What are they doing there?'

Johnnie pulled his 'I dunno' face.

'I dunno. But if you're going back in time you may as well visit one of the Seven Wonders of the Ancient World.'

I looked at the little face on the Sphinx. People described it as having the body of a lion, with the head of man. But I always thought it looked like a girl's face. Actually, I always thought it looked

like *my* face. But don't tell anybody that. They might think I'm big-headed.

But I put that thought out of my mind. Because something else was puzzling me.

'Hold on. If they're *there*, how did the shoe and the tree get *here*?'

LiterALLy Big-heADDeD! iNteresting fAct: the GreAt SphiNx's eArs Are oNe metre LoNg

JohNst x

'So what are we going to do?'

I needed to take charge. That much was pretty clear.

'OK, Johnster, in two days we're dead meat. We need to get this time machine built. I'm gonna help you.'

'Thanks, 'Liza. It's really hard, you know.' Johnnie looked so relieved it made me feel guilty.

'So,' I said, 'how do we actually build this thing?'

HOW TO ACTUALLY BUILD
A TIME MACHINE

Back inside Dad's workshop, Johnnie showed me
what he'd been doing for the last twenty-four hours.

'So that's where the new sofa went,' I said lamely.

Johnnie whipped away some of the cushions.

'Cool, huh?'

'Yeah, I guess. But how does it actually work?'

'Easy.' Johnnie scribbled on a new piece of paper and handed it to me. 'You just need four things.'

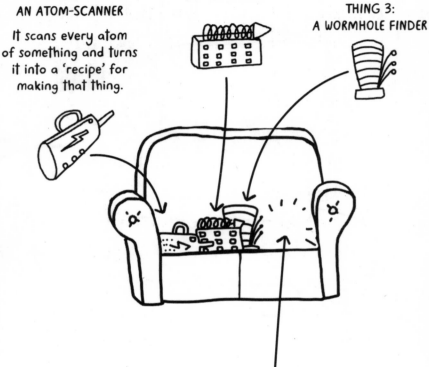

THING 2:
AN ATOMIC 3D PRINTER

It reads the recipe and 'prints' the thing atom by atom on the other side of the wormhole.

THING 1:
AN ATOM-SCANNER

It scans every atom of something and turns it into a 'recipe' for making that thing.

THING 3:
A WORMHOLE FINDER

THING 4:
AN OBLITERATOR

My head was spinning . . .

'Dad left almost everything we need,' said Johnnie, jigging up and down. 'The scanner, the 3D printer, the wormhole finder. The only thing missing is the obliterator.'

'What's that for?'

'Oh, it kind of obliterates us after the recipe has gone down the wormhole.'

'*Obliterates* us? As in totally destroys us?!'[10]

'Well, yeah, kind of.'

'Kind of?? Why do you need to do that?'

'So we don't end up with two of us.'

'Can't we just keep the old us as well?'

'Think of the negative energy.' Johnnie bit into an apple. 'You have to keep the universe in balance,' he added (as if that explained anything).

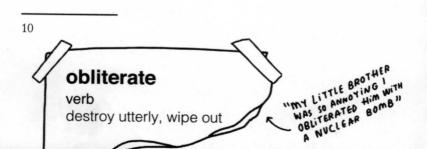

obliterate
verb
destroy utterly, wipe out

"MY LITTLE BROTHER WAS SO ANNOYING I OBLITERATED HIM WITH A NUCLEAR BOMB"

'So, if we make a Johnnie and Eliza in the past, we have to destroy the Johnnie and Eliza in the now?'

'Yep, we have to obliterate them so—'

'Them? You mean *us*.'

'OK, obliterate *us*, but the recipe for *us* will be in the wormhole. So we'll be fine.'

That was when it suddenly struck me: Mum and Dad hadn't gone back in time, the *recipe* for Mum and Dad had gone back. The real Mum and Dad had been *obliterated*.

I burst into tears.

Johnnie just looked confused.

Then he put a hand out and I held it.

'Have the real Mum and Dad really been obliterated, then?' I finally asked.

Johnnie said, 'No,' but he nodded at the same time.

'OK,' I said, taking a massive breath. 'But promise you'll test it on something else first – an apple or something – before you try it on us, so we know it's safe?'

Johnnie pulled a face. 'I've already tested it – loads of times – but it always goes wrong.' He pointed at the workbench. It was covered in bits of junk, like a lawnmower had just exploded.

'Johnnie, is this the obliterator? It's all in bits.'

Johnnie's chin wobbled, but he managed a croaky little voice. 'I need more time, Eliza.'

By the looks of the workbench, he needed a decade.

'All right, Johnst.' I held his cheeks like Mum used to when he was upset. 'We've got two days. Is that enough?'

Johnnie shook his head.

We needed more time.

HOW TO MAKE TIME

We had two days until everyone turned up expecting a party, and Johnnie needed more time. Sadie was banking on the fact that I wouldn't be able to do it on my own.

She was banking on the fact that it would be a disaster and everyone would find out Mum and Dad were missing.

She was banking on the fact that organizing a Fancy Dress Garden-Skydiving party in *two* days would be totally impossible for someone like me.

But what if it wasn't a disaster?

What Sadie didn't know was, I wasn't *me* any more. I was **New Me**. I was the girl who'd crossed the Atlantic and saved a narwhal, stolen a rocket and defeated an evil billionaire. I was the Girl Who Never Gives Up.[11]

Dad called me that when I was a little baby, and he'd started again after we'd rescued him from Noah. And I must admit, after saving everybody, even I'd started maybe believing it. A little bit.

I got out a notepad and started to organize my thoughts:

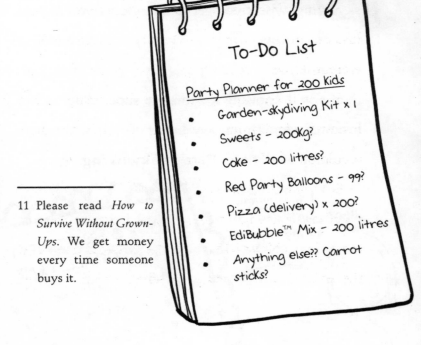

To-Do List

Party Planner for 200 kids
- Garden-skydiving Kit x 1
- Sweets - 200kg?
- Coke - 200 litres?
- Red Party Balloons - 99?
- Pizza (delivery) x 200?
- EdiBubble™ Mix - 200 litres
- Anything else?? Carrot sticks?

11 Please read *How to Survive Without Grown-Ups*. We get money every time someone buys it.

83

Now, depending on when you're reading this, you may be a bit confused about garden skydiving. If you're reading this before the year 2000, you might even think it's crazy impossible. But trust me, your games are rubbish, your toys are rubbish, and life's about to get a lot more fun.

If you're reading this *after* the year 2000, you'll know that someone super clever invented *indoor* skydiving: where you get to fly indoors over a giant fan. Pretty cool.

But, if you're reading this forty years after that, then you'll know that someone super-super clever invented something *way* better. Possibly the best invention of all time: **__Garden__ Skydiving.**

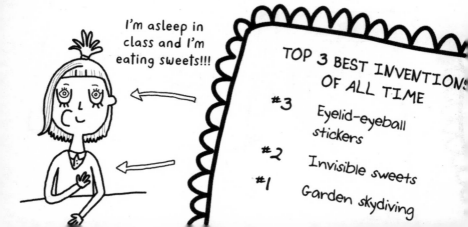

I'm asleep in class and I'm eating sweets!!!

TOP 3 BEST INVENTIONS OF ALL TIME

#3   Eyelid-eyeball stickers

#2   Invisible sweets

#1   Garden skydiving

The inventor's patent application had a diagram that looked like the one on the next page and, as soon as kids saw it, they literally went bonkers.

Now, this doesn't come cheap. And Sadie Snickpick was probably betting that no kid could ever afford to hire a garden-skydiving kit and set it up and not kill anyone. But I was determined. And I also had Mum's phone with all her credit cards stored in it.[12]

The garden skydiving was booked online in a few minutes. Delivery of 200 margherita pizzas was even easier. Then I just had to put 200 kilograms of sweets, 200 litres of coke, 99 red party balloons and 200 litres of EdiBuBBle™ mix into our shopping basket and check out.

---

12 Don't worry, *The Book of Secrets* has a chapter, **Secret 82: How to Break into your Mum's Phone.**

Job done. I didn't look at the price. Mum and Dad would understand. This party was a matter of life and death.

HOW TO HAVE THE BEST PARTY EVER

The next two days went by in a blur. Johnnie shut himself up in the workshop and spent every waking hour sweating over his obliterator. There was the occasional explosion, but mostly you could just hear him singing rock classics to himself.

Myrt and I spent the morning working on a playlist for the party.[13] Johnnie was looking stressed, so I gave him a tub of sweets. But that just seemed to make things worse. And then Myrt wanted a tub, and when Myrt wants something you just give it to her.

---

13 If you get the music right – a party's gonna be great. Get it wrong and you may as well serve parsley cake and write the whole thing off as a catastrophe.

And so, exactly two days after Mum and Dad had vanished, things were beginning to get a bit desperate.

How **NOT** to Survive Without Grown-Ups

OVERFLOWING WITH GUNKY DISHES

SWEETS FOR BREAKFAST

NOT TOUCHED IN DAYS

With a day to go, the garden-skydiving kit arrived. The people setting it up asked for my mum, but I just lied and said she had a migraine. It took them all afternoon, but finally, at about teatime, it was ready. They left, looking nervous, and told me to make sure my mum read the safety instructions before using.

But, with less than twenty-four hours until your life is doomed, there's no time for safety instructions. Even for me. I hit the **ON** switch and shouted for Johnster.

It was time to fly.

HOW TO FLY

I leaned forward over the first fan, and my cheeks quivered in the wind. I felt the fear, and then I remembered what it was like floating in space. Like a dream you never want to end. And I just had to trust the wind from the fan would lift me up and into the clear midsummer sky.

I leaned further forward, felt the rush as the wind began to lift me off my feet. I felt like a toddler in her dad's arms, flying round the bedroom.

And then I remembered: Dad was gone. And I fell flat on my face.

Someone had turned off the fans.

My nose was still jammed in the metal grill of the fan when I heard her voice. Sadie Snickpick's hate-filled voice. She sat on her bike, looking like she wanted to run me over.

'You just don't give up, do you, Eliza Lemon?'

I managed to get up without rubbing my sore face.

'No balloons?' Sadie sat there, smiling through her bubblegum.

'Mum and Dad are blowing them up tonight,' I lied. 'When they get back from work.'

'I can't *wait* to see them tomorrow,' she said sarcastically. 'Will they be dressing up too?'

I needed to stay calm. I needed to sound believable.

'They won't be here,' I said as casually as I could. 'They have to work. They work all the time, you know.'

Even I was impressed at how believable it sounded.[14] But Snickpick wasn't put off.

---

14 There's a whole chapter in *The Book of Secrets*, **Secret 55: How to Lie**. See Appendix 1.

'Your mum and dad are working on the day of your party? Well, I hope no one dies.'

She said it like she *wanted* someone to die. Like she was *planning* for someone to die.

'This is dangerous kit, you know.'

And, as if to make the point, she turned the fans back on, and shot me up into the air.

I flapped about, fighting my way back down to the ground. Sadie turned her bike round and rode off.

And I just knew, without any doubt whatsoever: this was going to be the *worst* party ever.

HOW TO SURVIVE A PARTY THAT'S A MATTER OF LIFE AND DEATH

The day of the party, I woke up feeling vommy. You know, when you wake up, and feel like pooh, but you don't remember why. And then you remember why. Well, it was exactly like that. But poohier.

NORMAL ME

VS

ME ON THE MORNING OF THE WORST PARTY EVER

Johnnie was nervous too. And that's always bad.

Myrt took one look at us arguing over breakfast, and slunk off to find Dad's hammock.

'What do you mean, you won't help? There are ninety-nine balloons to blow up. *Before* lunchtime!'

'But I'm nearly done. I've finished the obliterator; I just need to put everything together. We don't even need the party. We can just go this morning and miss it altogether.'

I had a vision of being obliterated at 11.59 a.m. by the time machine, just before everyone turned up. It was tempting. But not tempting enough.

'No, Johnster,' I said firmly. 'You need to test it before I go anywhere near that thing.'

'Fine,' said Johnnie. 'I will.' He grabbed an apple and disappeared through the kitchen door.

With Johnnie gone, the morning raced on. What they don't tell you before you blow up ninety-nine balloons is that having a foot-pump is only half the answer. Tying them up is the tricky bit. Tying one balloon is easy. Even ten. But after that your fingers enter a world of pain as the rubber crushes and bruises your fingertips.

By 11.50 a.m., when the last balloon was blown, tied and strung up, my hands felt like they'd been chewed by a cow.

Only ten minutes to go.

I got into my party outfit.

I tipped out the sweets into some buckets.

11.55 a.m.

Five minutes to go.

Five minutes till DOOM O'CLOCK.

Then Sadie Snickpick arrived, five minutes early. She hadn't bothered with fancy dress either.

'*Ciao!*'[15] she said, but the smirk on her said more.

---

15 It means 'hello' in Italian. Sadie Snickpick thinks it's cool to say *ciao*. She's a monster.

What we say vs what we mean

So much more.

She helped herself to a sweet and chewed slowly, waiting for me to answer.

I just stood there. Frozen like a runaway hamster whose little ball has rolled into the mouth of a cannon.

And then more people turned up. First a trickle, then more, and then finally hordes. It was like a football match. I could hear cars queuing up the road, doors slamming shut, and people just appeared in my garden, like mushrooms after a storm.[16]

I knew most of them, and I was swept away from Sadie Snickpick in a gust of 'Hello's and 'Help yourselves'. But not all the kids who turned up were from our school. Some were older. A lot older. A group of boys who must have been at least fourteen were shouting and laughing. And they soon had the skydiving machine turned on.

'The Twenty Minuters!' said a voice behind me, and I turned to see Sadie Snickpick.

'Twenty Minuters?'

'I give them twenty minutes before you have to call the first ambulance.'

---

16 I don't know if mushrooms do appear after a storm, but I just liked that sentence.

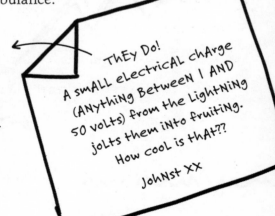

ThEy Do!
A smALL electricAL chArge
(ANythiNg BetweeN I AND
50 volts) from the LightNiNg
jolts them iNto fruitiNg.
How cool is thAt??

JohNst xx

I looked over at the older boys tossing younger kids into the skydiving zone. Twenty minutes was possibly being generous. Seven-year-olds were flying around like helium balloons. And now more people were turning up. One of the boys tipped a bucket of sweets on to the fans and everyone screamed as great plumes of sweets billowed about like clouds.

Everyone went nuts. Flying sweets are just too. Much. Fun.

The Twenty Minuters

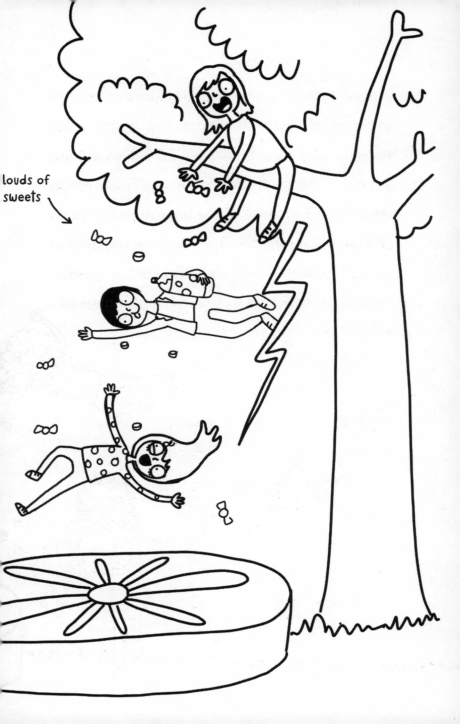

louds of
sweets

And then the worst possible thing of all – a grown-up arrived with a scared-looking Year 2 girl. It was a dad, thank goodness. He looked around, not sure what to do. Stern, but terrified all at the same time. Then he kissed his daughter and did a runner. Thank God it was a dad and not a mum.

'One minute down, nineteen to go.' Sadie Snickpick counted down, like the devil, in my ear.

All I could do was watch. And, sure enough, right on twenty minutes, the first fan exploded in a shattering arc of electricity. Someone had jammed it with sticks to see what would happen. It cracked like thunder, and the first children started crashing down from the sky, like dead aeroplanes.

In the middle of all this, Myrt arrived, carrying something in her mouth. She dropped it at my feet.

An apple.

A manky, rotten apple.

I just stared at it, and then I suddenly knew what it meant. Johnnie had tested the time machine. He'd sent the apple back in time. And here it was now, rotten. The final proof we needed.

I looked down at the apple, all brown and puckered like an old man's bald patch. I looked up at Sadie Snickpick, then back at the rotten apple.

And I ran, Myrt close at my heels.

We ran to the workshop as if the devil herself was after us.

Which she was.

HOW TO TRAVEL IN TIME

I got to the workshop just as a second giant fan exploded. There were flames this time, but I was in the barn and had the door bolted behind me without taking a second look. Myrt had rushed in ahead of me, and was barking like mad.

Suddenly Sadie Snickpick came crashing against the timber, but the bolt held.

'You can't run away from this, Eliza Lemon!' she shouted through the wooden slats. 'No one can run from this!'

Johnnie was sitting on the sofa, hugging a backpack on his lap. Myrt jumped up next to him, wriggling like mad.

'Get on, 'Liza. It totally works!'

But then I remembered that word.

'**Obliterator.**'

This machine wasn't sending me back in time. It was obliterating me. And then sending back a recipe for me.

A recipe for my brain, but what about my mind? My memories and ideas and feelings and all the zillion things I'd ever imagined?? I wasn't just a recipe. I was a human being.

Wasn't I?

Another *THUMP*. Sadie Snickpick's shoulder came bashing against the barn door. Myrt started growling.

'Johnnie, this is mad. Why don't we just send the time machine back and then Mum and Dad can—'

Another crash, and this time Sadie's boot came smashing through the wood.

Time was up.

I looked at Johnnie. His long eyelashes sparkled

with tears. I thought about the mayhem outside: children crashing to the ground, ambulances arriving with flashing lights, Sadie Snickpick laughing as they trapped Myrt in a cage and drove her away. Maybe they'd do that to Johnnie and me too.

Sadie's boot pulled back. One more kick and she'd be through. We'd blown it. We'd failed. *I'd* failed.

And then I thought, *Everyone needs a second chance now and again. A do-over. Maybe sometimes it is better to be obliterated and start again. Maybe sometimes you can rewrite the past.*

I jumped on to the sofa like I'd done a thousand times before. But maybe for the last time.

'Go-go-go-go-go-go!' I shouted.

Johnnie hit PLAY on his little remote control. An electric motor started whining beneath my cushion. I gripped on to Myrt, terrified she'd jump away and be left behind.

But then, before anything could happen, the barn door came smashing open. Sadie Snickpick had virtually kicked it off its hinges. The view into the garden was like a disaster movie.

All I could think as Sadie walked slowly towards us was, *Get away from me.* But my mouth just wouldn't work. And, even if it had, I doubt it would have made much difference.

Sadie Snickpick had a smirk of curiosity, a look, almost, of respect. Almost.

'What are you up to?' she said with genuine interest. 'You don't actually have some plan to get out of this mess, do you?'

Three seconds more and we'd have won. We'd have been hurtling back into the distant past to save our mum and dad, ready to come back and stop the party-from-hell ever happening.

But Sadie Snickpick has a bully's instinct for

knowing exactly when to poke a stick into the spokes of your bike wheel. I'd seen her send a dozen kids flying over their handlebars. And, with a bully's instinct, she leapt on to the brown sofa.

She crashed on to me just as the atom-scanner whirred into action. A blue lattice of light passed over and through us all. And, seconds later, a robotic voice said two of the worst words in the English language:

'OBLITERATOR ENGAGED.'

And then, without any more warning than that, we were obliterated.

HOW TO BE OBLITERATED

The only way I can describe it is like this: it's like being microwaved and tumble-dried and farted on all at the same time.

I grabbed Johnnie's sticky hand, even though Sadie's elbow was grinding into my face. And the next moment, like waking from a daydream, everything was the same and different all at the same time.

Sadie's elbow was still in my face. Johnnie's chubby hand was still a bit sticky. But the barn was gone. Everything was gone: house, garden, party, flying children, exploding machines, broken children. Everything. We were still on the sofa; Johnnie was still clutching the backpack on his lap like an old lady with her handbag on a bus. I pushed Sadie away; she looked like she wanted to bite me.

And then I noticed.

There was one really big difference.

The sofa was stuck at the top of a tree.

To be more precise, it was stuck at the top of a rainforest.

'Who farted?' said Sadie, looking at Johnnie.

You have to give it to her, she'd just been obliterated and rebuilt up a tree in 5000 BCE, and she still wanted to pick a fight. Some people are just born that way, I guess.

'No one,' said Johnnie with a huge smile. 'That's just the smell of ozone from the plasma trail.'

She thought he was making fun of her, and cuffed him on the side of the head. The sofa rocked and a branch creaked angrily.

'What have you idiots just done?' She stood up to

take a better look around. 'What the . . . ?'

There was no word in the English language that could (adequately) end that sentence. No word that could come close to expressing what she could see.

Johnnie and I carefully climbed up on to the back of the sofa, and we saw it too.

WHAT THE . . . ?

'Where are we?' Sadie asked Johnnie.

'We've gone south-east and back,' he said simply, 'by about two thousand miles and 7,053 years.'

'The Sphinx,' I said faintly, 'is it supposed to look like that?'

The Great Sphinx of Egypt, the First Wonder of the Ancient World, looked like it had been coloured in by a two-year-old.

'And look,' said Johnnie, smiling as if he'd just made the discovery of the century. 'It's got a lion's head.'

'The Sphinx used to be a big lion?'

'Looks like it.'

'Why is there jungle in Egypt anyway?' Sadie reached out to touch some leaves. 'And the pyramids? Where are the pyramids!?'

'I guess they're not built yet,' said Johnnie.

Sadie Snickpick, possibly for the first time in her

entire life, looked a bit lost. But it didn't last long, less than a second, and then Angry Face was back.

She snatched the remote from Johnnie without another word, and started jabbing at the fast-forward button. There was a whirr deep within the sofa. Something was moving.

And then nothing.

'How does it work?' she said, looking at the remote.

'Just press the volume up button. The more you press it, the more it scans,' Johnnie said, not unhelpfully.

'Make it work!' Sadie shouted, and chucked the remote at Johnnie. It hit him on the forehead and he collapsed with a howl.

I don't know what happened after that. Maybe, after years of being bullied, I wasn't going to let Johnnie be bullied too. Maybe I'd just had enough of Sadie Snickpick and wanted to put an end to all her misery.

But mostly I just wanted to strangle her.

I launched myself right at her, right at Sadie Snickpick's throat.

We were 7,000 years in the past. There were no grown-ups to step in and sort this one out.

This was going to be **the fight to end all fights**.

And I knew exactly what I needed to do to win it.

HOW TO WIN A FIGHT

The Book of Secrets has a chapter that explains everything: *exactly* how to win any fight,[17] even against someone who's bigger and stronger and savager than you.

My only problem was that despite reading the chapter loads of times, and even practising a bit on my cousins, none of it had ever really stuck in my brain. And what had stuck completely disappeared the second I launched myself at Sadie Snickpick's throat.

I thought about asking for a 'T-out' so I could get the book out of Johnnie's rucksack. But I only

---

17 See **Secret 139: How to Win a Fight.**

thought of that *after* I'd leapt at her.

Now that I've had the chance to reread that chapter, I realize that in this, my First-Ever-Proper-Fight, I made three crucial mistakes.

Basically, it ended when Sadie Snickpick almost pulled my head off. The whole time we were fighting, I was terrified that she'd chuck me off the sofa and I'd die, falling into the jungle below. At one point, she almost scalped me, with just her fingernails. They were like claws, and she fought like an animal. But then Myrt got involved and she fought like an animal too. I managed to squirm free just before my head went pop.

I immediately tripped, falling backwards. I thought I was a goner, but I landed on the edge of the sofa. Sadie stood on me, pinning me down with one leg. She grabbed Johnnie, lifting him right into the air.

As I lay there, with Sadie's footprint still on my

BICEPS =

CHIMPANZEE STRENGTH

face, I remember thinking, *God, she's strong. She's like an ape.*

'Get this thing working, you little numb-nut.' She shook Johnnie like a toy doll.

'I can't! We need to recharge it,' Johnnie spluttered.

And then, with a crack like a breaking branch, the branch broke. And the sofa plunged into the jungle below.

We clung on like surfers riding the wave of our lives.

HOW TO SURF A SOFA

It never really picked up speed, which helped. We thumped into a solid trunk after about three metres. We'd have been flung off, but the web of branches was thick around us. Johnnie would still have managed to fall, except Sadie Snickpick had him gripped by the T-shirt.

The remote, on the other hand, wasn't so lucky. It slid, then spun, tumbling over the side, shredding leaves as it picked up speed on its way to the forest floor.

Johnnie wailed in despair. But Sadie didn't miss a beat.

'I guess we need that thing.'

Johnnie nodded, still in her impressive grip.

'Well then,' she said, releasing Johnnie at last, 'let's get down there.' She kicked out at a branch and I heard it crack, and then we were moving again, faster this time. And this time Johnnie did fall. He just slipped off the side.

I saw him go, his little mouth wide open in horror and his arms flapping like a baby bird.

And then came the sickening sound, as the meat and bones of his body smacked into branches all the way down. I looked over the side and saw him, my broken little brother, flat out on the jungle floor.

I screamed at Sadie, but she'd taken a bang. A bang to the head that seemed to have knocked all the sense out of her. I took the opportunity to call her a 'stupid cow' right to her face. But I was too worried to enjoy it.

I needed to get to Johnnie and, without thinking too much, I started hammering at the branches with my foot. Lashing out with all my strength until another branch gave way, and we started our final plunge to the forest floor.

You probably think we were lucky not to land on Johnnie. That just shows you've never surfed a sofa down through a rainforest canopy. The tangle of vines and branches keeps you permanently moving

The Physics of Jungle Sofa Surfing

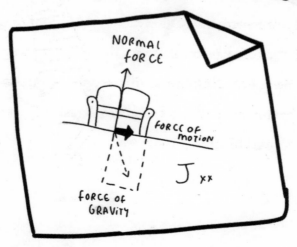

crossways. Like a surfboard sliding along a wave.
So, by the time we hit the forest floor, we were
twenty metres away.

I was shaken by that last drop, but was up and
running over to Johnnie in a second. And, when I
got to him, my worst fears came crashing over me.
He looked terrible.

'Is he all right?' asked a voice behind me.

I sat him up, and he grunted, pupils weirdly small, like he'd banged them shut when he hit the ground. He didn't look like Johnnie and he didn't sound like Johnnie; words were mumbling out of him like he was sleep talking. Then he blinked and his eyes seemed to go back to normal; he spoke in his normal voice too, and I just knew everything was going to be OK.

'Look over there,' he said, his voice reassuringly steady. 'I think that thing really wants to kill us.'

HOW NOT TO BE KILLED BY A THING THAT REALLY WANTS TO KILL YOU

'Or maybe it's just a mock charge,' finished Johnnie.

I spun round and saw it immediately. A huge animal, head low, nostrils wide.

Like a giraffe but without the neck, I remember thinking. I know what *you're* thinking: a giraffe is *defined* as an animal with a long neck. So an animal without a long neck can't look like a giraffe. But I'm guessing you've never travelled 7,000 years into the past and been attacked by 'Shiva's Beast'. Aka the Sivatherium.

Giraffe vs Sivatherium
(you say it Sheeva-thir-ree-um)

It snorted as it ran, head lurching side to side as it charged right at us. The acceleration as it smashed through the forest made my heart leave my body. I grabbed Johnnie, and some instinct made me bury him in my chest. He squealed, complaining, but I pushed him down to the ground, smothering him with my body. I wasn't going to lose him twice in one afternoon.

The hooves drummed a beat as they thundered across the earth. Louder and louder. If this was a mock charge, it was a lot more convincing than it needed to be.

I couldn't help looking up. And there was the stampeding beast, seconds away from crashing over us. Head down, eyes shut, nostrils wide in a bellowing snort. The horns looked heavy and blunt. Like a caveman's club.

If I shut my eyes, even now, I can see its head hurtling towards us, like the world's scariest GIF playing a loop in my head.

But the GIF in my head plays on for two seconds more.

WORLD'S SCARIEST GIF (GIF.RAFFE?)

SADIE SNICKPICK'S
HAND? HOLDING A
SMALL STICK??

After ten seconds, I realized three very important

things about Sadie Snickpick:

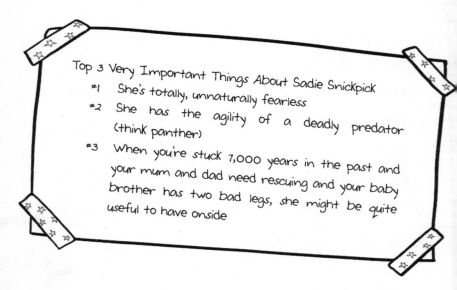

Top 3 Very Important Things About Sadie Snickpick
*1   She's totally, unnaturally fearless
*2   She has the agility of a deadly predator
      (think panther)
*3   When you're stuck 7,000 years in the past and
      your mum and dad need rescuing and your baby
      brother has two bad legs, she might be quite
      useful to have onside

Despite everything, despite all the fear raging

through me, I suddenly knew something. Something

I should have realized long ago (or long in the future,

now I think about it). There was something *different*

about Sadie Snickpick.

Something *not quite natural*.

I looked at the Sivatherium crumpled in a heap on the ground. I thought it might be dead, but it soon sprang up and ran away. I looked at Sadie Snickpick with fresh eyes. No one had the reflexes and the timing and the sheer speed of thought to do that. To tug a charging animal right in the left nostril while it's charging straight at you? Even the greatest bullfighter who ever lived[18] couldn't have done that. It just wasn't humanly possible.

I looked at her dusting off her trousers, and felt a shudder. What if she wasn't completely human? No, that's absurd, I shook the thought away and forgot it almost immediately.

---

18 The greatest bullfighter who ever lived was actually a man called Carlos Fandango. He was so light-footed he could (famously) climb a set of stairs without touching them! (No, it's not impossible, you just ping off the walls.) He's my hero for introducing the world to vegan bullfighting. Aka bull-dancing-until-they-get-dizzy-and-fall-over.

Johnnie was hurt, Myrt too. I carried them both back to the sofa.

Myrt's leg was in a bad way; she growled when I tried to take a look and then lay down for a good ol' chew on it. Johnnie's leg was worse. *Much* worse. He made a ton of fuss. You'd have thought it had come off. Sadie Snickpick listened to him for a whole minute before she'd had enough.

'Does it hurt?' she asked.

Johnnie nodded.

'Then it's not broken. Everyone knows that. Just sit down and shut up or I'll break the other one. I need to think.'

I left them to look for the remote. It was like everyone had forgotten that it was the only way out of this mess. But the light was failing, and with the night would come new dangers. Soon I had to switch to finding wood for a fire, and turning the sofa into a shelter. As usual, I had to do all the work.

Sadie Snickpick just sat there, brooding, like an ogre in a fairy story.

Even when I'd finished, shelter complete, fire set and ready to light, she just sat there in silence. I didn't dare say anything, but I was hungry and no one else seemed to be making supper, so I opened up Johnnie's rucksack.

'Johnnie, the only proper food in here is a pack of XXXtra Sharp™ Sherbet Lemons.'

'So?' Johnnie looked defensive. 'What did *you* bring?'

'Like, nothing. I was busy with the party, remember?'

Now normally this situation would have led to a full-scale, brother–sister screaming match. But Sadie Snickpick snatched the rucksack and started tipping it out on to the sofa.

'There's eggs,' she said, holding up some Tupperware.

Johnnie snatched it back.

'They're not to eat. They're my turtle eggs.'

'Johnnie?' I said, exasperated. 'What did you bring those for?'

Johnnie had stolen the eggs from a beach on Noah's secret island and he'd been in big trouble for it ever since.[19]

'And what's all this other junk?' said Sadie, prodding at Johnnie's stuff like it was diseased. 'This is totally useless.' She held up a bamboo spoon to make the point. 'A baby spoon??'

Johnnie snatched it back.

'It's my Swiss Army spoon.'

But Sadie wasn't done, and her eyes widened in disbelief as she pulled out a large stalk of Brussels sprouts. 'You filled up most of your rucksack with sprouts?'

Johnnie snatched those back too. 'It's a survival vegetable.'

---

19 In case you don't know, stealing giant leatherback turtle eggs from a beach is not only illegal and against all the laws of nature, it's also really, really cruel because the turtles probably won't survive. And, even if they do, they won't know how to meet other turtles for mating and stuff. And these ones had been in space so they were probably all scrambled anyway.

'Sprouts?!'

'Yeah, sprouts. You can live on just sprouts for a month.' He waggled the stalk in her face. '*And* you can use it as a weapon.'

Sadie snatched it and smacked him on the nose.

'Oh yeah,' she said, satisfied by the random act of violence.

She went back to the rucksack.

'Is that purple flour? Hold on –' she pulled out a lemon, and a little bottle of glycerine – 'you've got the ingredients for a cake?!'

She tipped the rucksack out on to the sofa.

'Garlic? Garlic cake?? You weirdo. Are you worried about vampires?'

Johnnie had gone red in the face and was struggling to get everything back in his rucksack. He stuck some of the garlic in his mouth and started chewing.

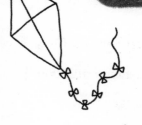

JOHNNIE'S RUBBISH STUFF

Child's kite

Stunt yo-yo

Water bottle

Mini-torch

Brussels sprout stalk

Dad's old shoe

The Book of Secrets

My new journal?

Cake ingredients?

Two turtle eggs in a Tupperware box

 Lemon (waxed)

XXXtra Sharp™ Sherbet Lemons (2 x packs)

 Flour (purple?)

Glycerine

 Aluminium foil

Garlic

 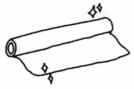

'It's to put off mosquitoes.'

'Gross,' said Sadie, and backed away.

'Why is the flour purple, Johnst?' I asked quietly.

'It's not flour, it's potassium permanganate.'

I must have looked blank because he then added, 'For sterilizing water.'

'Nice,' I nodded and he looked pleased.

And then he whispered, 'Did you see? I brought your new journal as well. I knew you'd want it.'

I took his hand silently, and gave it a little squeeze.

Sadie seemed to lose interest after that. The sun was setting and no one had much energy for arguing. I lit the fire, and Johnnie got comfy next to Myrt in one corner of the sofa. That left me and Sadie sucking sherbet lemons in an awkward silence.

There was a patch of night sky above us, a perfect circle packed with stars. They were strangely reassuring. We might be thousands of years lost

in time, but the stars were the same as they'd always been.

What's a few thousand years to a star, eh? I thought.

'Do you think there are any aliens up there having a really bad day too?' I said out loud without meaning to.

Sadie grunted; she was trying to get a stone out of her boot.

'I mean, on a planet going round one of those stars there could be three alien kids and an alien dog who have just gone 7,000 years back in time and are having a really rubbish adventure. And all we can see is their sun, twinkling away like it's always done.'

Sadie didn't look up from her boot. Silence makes me nervous, so I kept on talking.

'Did you know, those stars are thousands of light years away, so we're seeing thousands of years back in time whenever we look at a star.'

Sadie finally looked up from her boot.

'Yeah, so they've probably blown up by now. The universe doesn't care about me and I don't care about the universe.'

She was just being Sadie, but it did make me think. I could do a million different things here on Earth and the universe wouldn't even notice. And just then, at that exact moment, the star I happened to be looking at disappeared. I mean it literally vanished as I was looking at it.

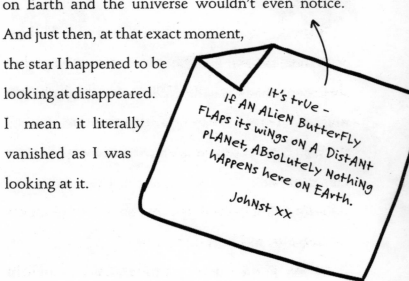

It's true – If AN ALieN ButterFLy FLAps its wiNgs oN A DistANt PLANet, ABsoLuteLy NothiNg hAppeNs here oN EArth.

JoHNst xx

'Whoa, the star I was looking at just *DIED*. It just went out.' I had the sudden heart-thumping thought of a billion aliens all dying as their star went black.

'Well, at least someone's having a worse day than me,' said Sadie. I could tell she just wanted me to shut up, so I did.

We sat in silence for a bit.

'D'you know, Eliza,' Sadie said eventually, 'if every one of those trillion stars had a planet with aliens living on it, you'd still be the biggest loser in the galaxy.'

'Sadie, why do you always have to be such a cow?'

'Why d'ya think, loser?'

'Mum says it's because your parents are toxic.' Johnnie's sleepy little voice sprang out of the dark to answer Sadie's question. 'Mum says bad parents make bad kids and she says your mum and dad are so busy making money they must be the worst parents ever.'

I held my breath. Johnnie has no idea when to keep his mouth shut.

But Sadie just snorted.

'And what does your dad say?'

'He says it's because you were born on the twenty-ninth of February and you're angry about the missing birthdays.'

'Oh, great, so you weirdos have got a whole list.'

We did actually have a list, but I wasn't going to admit it. And, thankfully, Johnnie kept his gob shut.

We sat there in silence for a bit. Until Sadie made a kind of angry grunt.

'You know, your mum and dad aren't any better than mine. Just because they tell you you're special all the time and treat you like a little princess.'

Maybe it was just the firelight, but I'd never seen Sadie looking so angry. I'd never seen *anything* looking that angry.

4 Reasons why Sadie Snickpick is a Humongous Bully.
#1 Dad's Theory: She was born on 29th February
#2 Mum's Theory: Mean Parents = Mean Kids
#3 Johnnie's Theory: She can't fart - Sloths can't fart and look how grumpy they are
#4 My Theory: She's a genetically modified psycho super-bully from the future, sent back in time to make my life totally miserable

'Just shut up. Your mum and dad left you. Remember that. It's because of them we're stuck here and it's because of them we're gonna die here.'

'Naaah, Mum'll sort it all out,' Johnnie piped up again from where he was lying at the far end of the sofa. We both turned, me in horror. He just didn't know when to keep quiet. 'Mum can basically do anything,' he finished, leaving a deathly silence.

Sadie's nostrils grew big, and for one horrible moment I thought she'd grab him again. But she just breathed in and out, staring at him like he was cat poo. Myrt's head bobbed up, but only for a second. She sniffed the air, seemed to decide everything was OK, and then flopped back down on Johnnie's lap.

Johnnie shut his eyes again, and I decided it was safest to join him. Squeezing up next to him and Myrt, careful to give Sadie a whole half of the sofa, I shut my eyes. I fell asleep to the sound of a knife grinding at bits of stone in Sadie's boot, calculating the hours we'd need to find a lost remote in a remote forest lost in time.

HOW TO FIND A REMOTE
IN A REMOTE RAINFOREST

The short answer is: don't even try.

It was small, black and not even shiny;[20] we could have spent 7,000 years looking for that remote and never found it. Besides, it had rained all night and we were soaked through. I woke, tired and wet and irritable. Something had bitten my ankle in the night and it had gone lumpy and so crazy-itchy I wanted to scratch my foot off. But I didn't.

---

20 Come on, people in companies – make them massive and yellow so you can't lose them.

ScieNce FAct:
IF you ADD up the time speNt every yeAr Across PLANet eArth LookiNg For sMAll BLAck remote coNtroLs it comes to 7,000 LiFetimes!

JohNst X

After one night, there was no argument about what to do. It was obvious. Dad's shoe told us to solve the riddle of the Sphinx. We had to get out of the rainforest, get to the Sphinx, and find Mum and Dad. And, anyway, we couldn't survive another night. Out here we were just bug food.

But if we could find Mum and Dad then everything would be all right. It had to be. And, like it or lump it, we'd need all the help we could get. And by lump it I meant Sadie Snickpick.

Bug Food = gruB gruB? 😂 J XX

Johnnie, stop writing in my journal. Your jokes aren't funny!

We showed Sadie the shoe. We explained everything. She didn't seem surprised, but then nothing ever seemed to surprise Sadie. Maybe she doesn't have the facial muscles for it. It didn't take her more than a second to decide what to do.

'They made this mess. They can sort it out,' she

said, lacing up her boots. 'Your useless parents can't be as useless as you two. What sort of idiot doesn't have a spare controller for their time machine?'

Johnnie started coughing uncontrollably. He'd got through to the fizzy bit of a sherbet lemon, and that always makes him cough.

Now, sweets for breakfast sounds GREAT, until you actually try it. After two sherbet lemons, my stomach felt like a sack of acid. I was almost tempted to try a raw sprout.

'But how do we get Johnnie's leg through the jungle?' I asked Sadie in a whisper.

'Duh. Use a stick and get him to lean on his good one?'

'But that is his good leg.'

I started to explain about Johnnie's weak left leg, but Sadie just held up a hand.

'OK, losers, you stay here and starve. I'm off.' And

without another word, she snatched up Johnnie's rucksack and left, disappearing into the rainforest with terrifying speed.

I looked at Johnnie, and back in the direction of Sadie Snickpick as she stomped her way through the jungle.

'Johnnie, I'll get her back,' I said, but he wailed at me.

'Don't go, 'Liza. We'll figure something out. We have to stick together. Together we're an ocean, remember?'

Myrt sat up, knowing something was wrong. She always barked when we argued, and she did now.

'Johnst, you'll be fine for five minutes. Myrt'll stay and I'll be back in two seconds. We can't let Sadie go without us. She's got the bag with all the stuff.'

He was starting to cry, and Myrt was howling.

But there was no point arguing. I knew I should stay, but I had to go. If I left it any longer, I'd lose Sadie completely, and then we'd all be doomed.

'Johnnie, two seconds, OK?'

I ran after Sadie Snickpick.

HOW TO CATCH A BULLY

Sadie was smashing her way through the jungle with a big stick, and the noise carried. I followed the sound, shouting the whole time. But she was fast, and I struggled to keep up.

And then, after what must have been no more than a minute,[21] I lost her.

I turned, but my stomach flipped. No matter where I looked, the jungle was the same. Like the trees had moved to cover my way back.

I felt myself start to panic, and I shouted, 'Johnnie!'

I waited for an answer. But nothing. So I shouted again.

---

21 OK, it may have been more like five minutes but definitely no longer than that.

'Johnnie! Myrtle!!'

Still nothing.

If you think getting lost in a rainforest in under five minutes is ridiculous, then you've never been in a rainforest. And I was pretty sure this one hated me. It was just so ridiculously easy to get lost. You get turned around trying to fight your way through until you've no idea whether back is forward or forward is back. No matter how loudly I shouted or screamed, the sound just came bouncing back at me. Once or twice, I thought I heard Myrt barking, but it could've been anything.

I don't think that makes sense
Jxx

I spent most of the morning running and tripping and running. Getting tangled and bitten and stung. At one point I caught something actually trying to eat my ear. It was a huge beetle thing that

149

somehow got into my hair and thought I wouldn't notice when it started eating me. Freaky doesn't even half cover it. The faster I tried to run, the worse everything got.

Until, by some miracle, I heard someone shout. My name.

'Eliza!'

Sadie's voice. She sounded angry, but she always sounds angry. She sounded like she was bashing her way through the jungle with a big stick.

'Sadie!' I shouted, running towards the noise.

But then the worst possible thing happened.

The noise stopped. And almost immediately I didn't know where to go.

I held my breath and listened, desperate to hear anything. And the jungle, after being as noisy as a bouncy-castle party all morning, was suddenly quiet. Even the birds had stopped.

'Sadie!' I shouted again. But still nothing.

So I shouted again. And again, and again.

But nothing.

And then I fell through some massive jungle ferns. I literally tripped and fell and saw her.

Sadie Snickpick was standing with her back to a tree, facing me. She had one finger against her lips, and my heart leapt, but not with relief. Because on Sadie Snickpick's face was something I never thought I'd see. And that sight shoved an icy fist into my heart.

Because Sadie's eyes were wide with terror.

She waved an arm at me, slow and quiet as if to say, 'Get down and get away.'

Then I heard a gentle whoosh and a slap.

Something stuck in the back of her hand.

Something small and feathery.

A dart.

Poison blow dart? I remember thinking, but then Sadie's eyes grew big.

She toppled forward without a word. Slap-bang on to her fat face. I thought about helping her, and I thought about running. But, most of all, I didn't think at all.

Then I felt a stab in my head. Right on the bone of my forehead. I reached up and felt the skin twang as I pulled the dart out of my head. There was a fuzzy tingling down my left cheek, like you get at the dentist.

And then, well, I don't remember anything after that.

HOW TO SURVIVE A
POISON BLOW DART

My head felt like an ice-cream scoop was digging out my brain. My breath caught with the sudden pain, but then I remembered my kidnap training from *The Book of Secrets*[22] and kept my eyes shut, pretending to still be unconscious.

I was comfortable – that's the first thing I noticed. Lying on my back, on what felt like dry leaves. There were no ropes – I could move my hands and feet – so I risked squinting open one eye.

I expected a cage or something, but there was nothing. I was up on some kind of wooden platform. It even had a little roof. A bunch of parrots were

---

22 See **Secret 77: How to Get Out of School.**

sitting on it, right above my head, and I remember thinking, *How often do parrots poo?*

I opened my other eye, just a smidge, and looked out. The leaves were dry and brown, and I was on a thick mattress of them. Next to me, Sadie lay slumped on the ground. She was snoring like an elephant seal and, despite everything, I smiled.

Then a parrot landed on me and almost gave me a heart attack. Somehow it could smell the sherbet lemons in my pocket and had started pecking about. I tried shooing it away, but it just kept gently pecking.

I turned to get it off, terrified I'd be spotted. And that's when I saw.

And what I saw gave me the biggest jolt of my life.

A group of people, all on their knees, bending low. For a moment, I thought they were looking for something. Like they'd all dropped something. Or maybe they were in some Stone Age gym class.

And there was a drum; it started beating out a steady rhythm, louder even than Sadie Snickpick's walrus snore.

DUM, dum-dum-dum.

DUM, dum-dum-dum.

The beat somehow woke up my brain, and in the next moment I knew exactly what was happening. It's hard to describe how I knew it, but I did.

This wasn't Stone Age yoga.

This was *prayer.*

This was worship.

And it looked like . . . *I was the god.*

No, that was just some dumb movie plot. In real life you don't get to become a god just by travelling 7,000 years back in time, do you? Who was I kidding?

But then, as I listened to Sadie Snickpick snoring away, my brain tingled with a single delicious thought: the thought of Sadie Snickpick's face when she woke up and saw this. Because, now I watched more, it was all so obvious what was going on.

I was **the Chosen One**.

I was a GOD.

And then I remember thinking, *If they* think *you're a god, then you* are *a god*. You just need one person to believe. And, from the look of things, I had about twelve.

If Mum and Dad could see me now, I thought, and cleared my throat. With a dozen worshippers (followers? believers? devotees? I could decide later what to call them . . .), it would be dead easy to rescue Mum and Dad. Gods have everything easy. There's nothing they (we) can't do.

I sat up, and the parrot stopped pecking at my pocket and settled on my head. Its claws scratched and tangled in my hair and I felt panic rising.

Whether I wanted to or not, it was time for me, Eliza Lemon, to become a god.

HOW TO BE A GOD

I stood, ready to accept my worshippers. Practising my smile. And immediately realized that I'd got completely the wrong end of the stick.

And the other end of the stick was on fire.

Just occasionally, reality is worse than my imagination.

I wasn't a god at all.

I was a human sacrifice.

I was about to be burned alive.

HOW TO BE BURNED ALIVE

So now I know how Joan of Arc felt.

But how she just stood there while the flames burned the hair off her skin, and how she didn't go mad when that skin started to sizzle like a piece of bacon, I have *no* idea.

The more obvious reaction to being burned alive, and the one I picked out pretty much immediately, was to scream like I was dying.[23]

The worshippers (killers? Stone Age assassins??) looked up in horror and the drums suddenly stopped.

I was starting to feel heat on my legs and I screamed again. Some of the children began to cry; they looked

---

23 Which I probably was.

genuinely terrified, scattering into the bushes.

The parrot still sat there on my head, unfazed, but my screaming must have woken Sadie, because she sat up at that point. More looks of horror from below, but this time, one of the people rushed forward and started putting out the fire, batting it with a stick.[24]

The rest was a bit of blur. Suddenly, having been trying to kill us one minute, now they couldn't do enough for us. There was a lot of bowing and whispering in a language that sounded like a song. They even carried Sadie down from the platform, and she must weigh a ton.

The people (Stone Agers? Stoners?) looked nervous. They wore animal skins, just like you'd imagine. Some were old; some were young. There

---

24 Yeah, I know, not exactly 999-stuff. But this was the Stone Age, and it worked.

were even kids. It was like a big family. Suddenly I thought of Johnnie, and felt my heart collapse into my stomach.

They'd stopped bowing, but were clearly waiting for us to say or do something. And, even though Sadie was properly awake now, her eyes seemed to be looking in different directions. This was down to me.

'We go Sphinx.' I said, pointing.[25]

They looked at me blankly, and for some reason I was determined not to let Sadie be the chosen one. It was time to act the big cheese.

'Chop-chop!' I said, sounding weirdly like my gran. 'We go Sphinx NOW!'

More bowing. There must have been more than ten of them, all quite short, all dressed in scraggy

---

25 **Secret 88: How to Speak any Language** always seemed a bit simplistic to be honest. You basically skip school language classes and just point.

animal skins, all looking terrified.

Then the smallest, a tiny little woman, who could have been ninety, stepped forward and said, 'Id,' in a shaky sing-song voice.

She touched her chest.

'Eliza,' I said, doing the same with my hand.

She bowed low, almost touching the ground. And I like to think that I would have gone down in history as a pretty cool and benevolent god, but just then Sadie managed to stand up, and, in a voice that cracked like thunder, she came out shouting.

'**We go Sphinx**,' she screamed, '**NOW!**'

From then on, it was pretty clear who was in charge.

Id and the rest of the Stone Agers fell over themselves helping us.

Some things obviously don't need translating if you shout loud enough.

And clearly **'We go Sphinx NOW!'**, was one of them.

HOW GO SPHINX NOW

In movies, people cut their way through the jungle with a big machete.

In real life, it's a bit easier than that. In real life, the tree canopy is so thick that basically nothing grows down low. You might get the odd patch of ferns, if there's a break in the trees, say, but that's about it. That was lucky because the Stone Agers had two big wooden parrot cages, full of birds.

The best thing about *this* rainforest was that there weren't any spiderwebs. I'd been in a rainforest before and, trust me, there's nothing much worse than web all over your face. This time round, the downside to no spiders soon became obvious.

Bugs.

Bitey bugs.

They just kept landing on my face and hands and arms to suck out another little bit of me for lunch.

I spent the rest of the morning slapping myself, and the Stone Agers mainly kept their distance. Id smiled fearfully at me every now and again, but that was about it. They'd sing occasionally, and sometimes they'd all touch the trunk of a tree like it was some kind of superstition.

The whole time I was praying myself, and to no god in particular, that Johnnie and Myrt were OK. I imagined them still sitting on the sofa, injured, unable to move and all alone. They'd be getting thirstier and thirstier. That was the thing I kept thinking about. You can't go twelve hours in the heat without water. And I had no idea how long we'd been gone.

Then it rained and I felt a bit better. Johnnie was

a genius; there's no way he could die of thirst in a rainforest. But after the rain the bugs came back. More bites. I even had bites on my bites now. That's the thing they don't tell you in jungle survival books[26] – you don't get eaten by a panther or ambushed by baboons, you just itch to death. Literally, itch – to – death.

I could only imagine what was happening to Johnnie:

SUCKING ON A
SHERBET LEMON

LITERALLY ABOUT TO SCRATCH
HIMSELF TO DEATH

CARRIED AWAY
BY ARMY ANTS

Before   **After**

---

26 Or maybe they do. I dunno, I've never read a jungle survival book.

The further we walked, the more hopeless it all seemed.

I thought about going back, but there was no way I'd find him. That was the truth of it. I'd left him to die. I tried asking the people, the Stone Agers, but they looked terrified the moment I opened my mouth. And Sadie was no use – she told me to shut up and stop worrying and we'd sort it all out when we got to the Sphinx.

So all I could really do was worry, and walk, and hope. Hope that when we got to the Sphinx, and to Mum and Dad, they'd sort everything out. I was owed a bit a helicopter parenting.

So we trudged through the forest for the rest of the morning, slapping away at mosquitoes, and pulling rainforest pets out of my hair.

I soon lost track of how long we'd been walking, but when we did catch glimpses of the sun we could see it was high and bright, so I guessed it was close to midday. It felt like we'd been walking for days, and I was finally about to give up hope when, suddenly, I caught a glimpse of red through the trees. First red, then blue and yellow.

It was the Sphinx, and it was close.

Close enough to see how truly massive it was; the great lion head stood right above the tallest jungle trees, and I could only imagine the desert beyond.

As we got closer, other things became clearer: the trees were full of wooden buildings, connected by ropes and bridges, like some kind of tree village. *This must be Giza*, I realized stupidly late. We were about to make the greatest archaeological discovery of all time: we were about to enter the Lost City of Giza. Home to the pyramids, home to the Sphinx. The city that guarded the great Sphinx's secret.

If I ever get back to the future, I remember thinking,
I'll be famous.

Then, through a gap in the trees, I saw movement.

I looked across at Sadie and gave her a meaningful nod.

'What?' she said. 'It's just more Stone Age grots.'

But it wasn't more people, it was just one. As we broke through the trees into a sunny clearing, I saw a boy. A boy no older than me.

Id, the old woman, shouted something and everyone collapsed to their knees. That's when I realized that the boy wasn't just a boy; he was a god, just like us.

And then the Boy-God spoke.

And, in one sentence, everything I knew about the world turned upside down.

'About time,' he said. 'What have you gumps been playing at?'

HOW TO MEET A BOY-GOD

Admit it, you had low expectations. You were probably expecting all Stone Age boys to look like this:

STONE AGE BOY (IN YOUR HEAD)

GRUNT

COMBS NOT INVENTED UNTIL 3000 BCE

OFFERS YOU A BOGEY[27]

HOME TO PARASITES INCLUDING EAR LICE AND BUM WORMS[28]

SCARY HAIRY

TOYS = STONES

(FIRST PROPER TOY NOT INVENTED UNTIL 4000 BCE)

---

27 In case you think this is rubbish, scientists believe that prehistoric humans used bogey-sharing as a way of protecting themselves from disease. Next time you eat one, think of bogeys as the 'World's First Vaccine'.

28 Yes, bum worms are an actual thing. They were a big problem back then.

And, to be honest, most of them did. But the Boy-God, well, he was something else. Something else entirely.

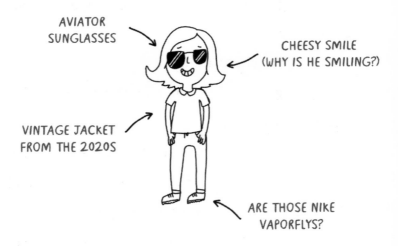

ACTUAL STONE AGE BOY

AVIATOR SUNGLASSES

CHEESY SMILE (WHY IS HE SMILING?)

VINTAGE JACKET FROM THE 2020S

ARE THOSE NIKE VAPORFLYS?

He pushed his glasses on to the top of his head with a big smile. And what he said next blew my mind even further apart.

'Come on, Johnster's been half worried to death.'

I never got to reply, because suddenly there was Johnnie, riding towards us on the short-necked giraffe, smiling like it was the most normal thing in the world. The Stone Agers dropped back to their knees, and then Myrt's head was peering round too, sitting behind Johnst. The Stone Agers bowed even lower.

I couldn't believe it.

'These guys will worship anything,' said Sadie, clearly annoyed too.

But I was too busy running towards Johnnie. I pulled him into my arms, said sorry a thousand times and crushed him with a hug. He smelled of old garlic, but I didn't care. I even let Myrt bite me in all the excitement.

'You're spilling my drink,' Johnnie said eventually, and I put him down.

'How's your leg?'

'Baaad.'

But he was doing his little hoppy up and down thing, so it couldn't be that bad.

I had a thousand questions, but most of all I just wanted to look at his little potato face. I tried to say sorry, but he kept jabbering on. In all the tears (mine) and explanations (his) I learned four things:

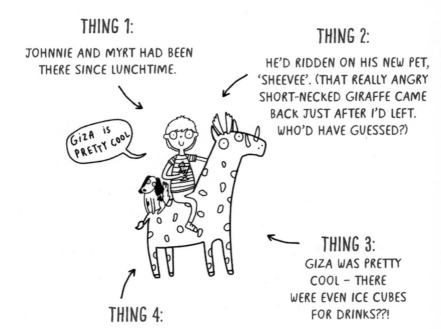

THING 1:

JOHNNIE AND MYRT HAD BEEN THERE SINCE LUNCHTIME.

GIZA is PRETTY COOL

THING 2:

HE'D RIDDEN ON HIS NEW PET, 'SHEEVEE'. (THAT REALLY ANGRY SHORT-NECKED GIRAFFE CAME BACK JUST AFTER I'D LEFT. WHO'D HAVE GUESSED?)

THING 3:

GIZA WAS PRETTY COOL – THERE WERE EVEN ICE CUBES FOR DRINKS??!

THING 4:

HIS GOOD LEG (WHICH WAS NOW HIS BAAAD LEG AFTER THE FALL) WASN'T TOO BAD ACTUALLY AND WAS 'KIND OF FINE'.

'Ice cubes?' I said in amazement at Johnnie's half-spilled drink. 'Where'd you get ice cubes?'

Johnnie looked at them as if he'd never thought about it.

'I guess they've got a freezer.' He smiled his little preschool smile. 'It's *amazing* here, 'Liza.'

I followed his eyes up into the trees. There were so many treehouses, with rope ladders and bridges everywhere.

'What are all the birds for?' I said, nodding at a sea of giant cages.

This was a topsy-turvy world all right. A world where people lived in trees and birds lived on the ground. And there were hundreds of them: birds, that is. Parrots in every colour you could imagine.

'Come and check out our treehouse,' said Johnnie.

And off he went, towards the edge of the jungle, expecting me to follow. And that was it, no screaming or shouting. No, 'I can't believe you left me in the jungle to die!'

Nothing.

Five-year-old boys are weird. It's like they can't hold a grudge. Not even for a minute.

Now, you're probably thinking what I was thinking. It's all very well Johnnie having a treehouse, but he was never gonna be able to climb up into it. Not with his bad leg. Not in a million years. It's why we'd never had bunk beds. ⬅

But it was increasingly obvious that these primitive Stone Age people were anything but primitive. They'd even invented the world's first lift.

THAt, AND the fAct thAt you screAm At me if I ever go iNto your BeDroom

J X

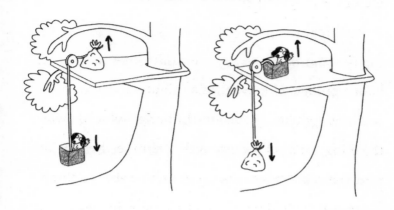

So that's how we got into Johnnie's treehouse.
It only had one storey, but that one storey was
amazing.

OK, not amazing-amazing, but pretty cool for 5000 BCE.

Sadie came up as well. And Boy-God joined us too, struggling to clamber up on to the treehouse floor, obviously a bit afraid of heights. I couldn't help wondering what he was doing here, 5,000 years in the past. But he looked pretty harmless, especially next to Sadie, so I decided (for once) to worry about him later.

Lunch came next, hoicked up in a big string bag from below.[29] It was cooked vegetables (mainly) and a kind of thick flat bread which sounds kind of grim when I write it down, but at the time, after a day of nothing but sherbet lemons, was great. The five of us ate lunch in silence. Johnnie's treehouse was right on the very edge of the jungle. It was like the ultimate ocean-view holiday room. Except it looked

---

29 Being a god is a bit like having parents to do everything for you, but without all the harassment.

on to endless desert, on to great, sweeping, shadowy sand dunes, like a beige ocean during a storm.

And the Sphinx was right there, so close I could have chucked a vegetable sandwich at it. Up close it looked a bit naff, all bright reds, and yellows and blues, like a three-year-old had painted it. But the eyes were wonderful; they sparkled dark green in the sun like the eyes of a giant cat.

'How long until they build the pyramids?' Sadie asked eventually, through a mouthful of bread.

The boy didn't answer – he just pointed to one of the dunes – the top of it glinted in the sunlight. And that's when I first noticed a line of Stone Agers trailing up to the top, and back down again. Like a string of ants, each one carrying a basket or pot. But it was only when I looked closely that I saw why.

Because there at the top, among all the birds, was a tiny flat-topped pyramid, no bigger than a kid's play tent, but glistening gold. Johnnie handed me his telescope.

IT LOOKS: MAYBE BIG,
BUT REALLY FAR AWAY??

... UNTIL A PARROT
LANDS ON IT

'It's tiny,' said Sadie, seeing the same thing as me. 'What are they doing? Feeding it and hoping it'll grow?'

'No, ya numpty, that's just the tip. It's buried,' said the boy.

'Is the whole thing covered in gold?' Sadie's eyes were suddenly big. 'We'll be the richest people, like, ever.'

'If you can find a rich enough fool to buy it off you,' said the boy taking a bite of his sandwich. 'It's just fool's gold.'

'Iron pyrite,' explained Johnnie. 'It just *looks like* gold.'

Sadie shrugged. 'So what are they chucking into it?'

'Guano,' said the boy, all matter-of-fact, 'AKA bird poo.' As if it was totally normal to do anything with bird poo.

'I suppose you've got to put it all somewhere,' said Johnnie, and he laughed, but everyone else went back to their vegetable sandwiches.

Sadie was the first to finish lunch – she eats like a carnivore, even when no meat is involved – and she asked the questions I'd been thinking about all along:

'So who are you? And what are you doing here?'

The boy smiled. 'I'm doing my history homework.'

Sadie snorted. 'History homework?'

'Yeah, we get one school trip a year, anywhere in time and space and—'

Sadie didn't let him finish. 'You're on a school field trip? To 5000 BCE?'

'The future sounds so cool,' Johnnie said through a mouthful of bread. 'Does everyone get a field trip?'

'Shut up, Johnnie,' said Sadie 'What's your name?'

The Boy-God looked a bit surprised by that.

'My name?' he said, finishing his sandwich. 'We don't have names. You don't really need them in the future.'

Sadie looked at me as if to say, 'Do you believe that?'

I just pulled a face. Would you really need a

name in the future?

'We just use a 256-bit crypto hash function because we communicate virtually.'

I looked at Johnnie; he was nodding. 'So everyone just has a unique string of numbers and letters? That's so cool.'

I looked back at the boy. The bites on my back were driving me crazy.

'Who wants ice cream?' he said abruptly, looking pleased with himself.

And, without waiting for an answer, he raised his hands above his head and clapped three times. Like some kind of ancient sultan or emperor.

There was immediate activity below, and we saw someone running out into the desert along the length of the Sphinx, a tall girl with long black hair. She ran fast, disappearing round the back.

Thirty seconds later, she'd returned, still running

fast, but carrying something – a tub.

'Did she just pull a tub of ice cream out of the Sphinx's butt?' asked Sadie.

Boy-God smiled. 'It's where we keep the freezer.'

Johnnie gave me a meaningful look, as if to say, 'I told you it was the Riddle of the Sphinx's Butt.'

And then, well, then all my questions bubbled out.

HOW LONG HAVE YOU BEEN HERE?

AGES.

IS YOUR TIME MACHINE BROKEN?

YEP.

HAVE YOU SEEN MY MUM AND DAD?

NOPE.

CAN YOU GET US BACK?

MAYBE.

After his grilling, it was the boy's turn to ask questions. Maybe I should have been suspicious, but he'd been honest with us, so we were honest with him. Not realizing what a huge mistake that would turn out to be. Besides, the ice cream had arrived and it was really good.

Johnnie had already told him most of it anyway. And I told him the rest, all about Noah, and the time machine and Mum and Dad and our rescue mission. Most of all, though, he wanted to hear about our sofa time machine.

After we'd finished, he thought for a bit, but eventually said:

'If you want to find your mum and dad, we need to go and get your time machine. We can use it to look for them.'

'What about yours?' said Sadie. 'Why don't we just use yours?'

'Mine's bust; the obliterator's blown. And then there's the energy problem.'

'Is that what the birds are for?' asked Johnnie, and the boy immediately smiled again. He was kind of cute when he smiled.

'Yeah,' said Sadie, 'what is all the bird poo for?'

Johnnie turned to Sadie. 'Bird poo and fool's gold are the two main ingredients of gunpowder.'

'Gunpowder?' said Sadie.

'Gunpowder.' The boy nodded. 'I'm burning the bird poo into saltpetre. Once I add the fool's gold, I'll have enough gunpowder to blast me back to the future.'

I looked at Johnnie, as if to say, 'Does it really work like that?'

But he was nodding, so obviously it did. Shows what I know – I thought you needed electricity and batteries and stuff.

'So that's what you're doing in the pyramid?' asked Sadie. 'Can we go and see?'

The boy shifted on the rug. 'Sure, but we gotta get your time machine first. It'll be hard to find, and the rain won't be doing it any good.'

He was looking straight at me, as if he expected an answer.

'I don't know where it is,' I said, almost laughing. The idea that anyone would agree to go back into that nightmare of a jungle and be bitten to itch-death was totally ridiculous, not to mention the fact that it would be like looking for a needle in a haystack.

'I do,' said Johnnie, and we all turned. 'What?' he said. 'If you want to find a needle in a haystack, you just need a magnet.'

'I don't think it works like that, Johnst,' I said softly.

'Yes, it does. Myrt's the magnet.' He looked down at her as she tongue-wrestled her bowl of ice cream. 'She can find anything.'

'That's settled,' said the boy. 'We gotta go now and make the most of the light.'

But Sadie wasn't having any of it. 'If you think I'm going back out into that stinking jungle, you're an idiot.'

For the first time, there wasn't a smile on the boy's face. Just a flash of anger that quickly disappeared.

'It needs all of us,' he said quietly. 'You're comin' too.'

All of a sudden the air felt heavy. Like a cloud had covered the sun (it hadn't, but that's how it felt). It was like one of those nature programmes where two elephant seals face off on a beach. An alpha face-off. And we all know how they usually end up.

For about a minute, they just stared at each other. How the boy lasted that long mystified me. But, eventually, even he had to blink.

'Fine, you need a bath anyway.'

I thought she was going to punch him, but he hadn't finished. 'We've got mud baths for yer insect bites.'

His smile was back.

'They stop the itches.'

So that's how I ended up saying goodbye to Johnnie for the second time in a day. He sat on his 'Sheevee', Myrt dashing round its legs, and a bunch of glum-looking Stone Agers lined up behind them. Boy-God had his own ride, some kind of camel by the looks of it. Johnnie led the way, back into the rainforest with a confident wave, like an old explorer from a black-and-white film.

I regretted not going with him, of course I did, but not for long. My bites were so bad I could hardly think. And, besides, thank the gods I did stay, because if I hadn't I'd be dead.

In fact, so would everyone, even you.

And I say that without any swagitude, because in actual fact it was Sadie Snickpick who solved everything.

Sadie Snickpick, it turns out, is a bit of a Sherlock.

HOW TO BE A BIT OF A SHERLOCK

At the last minute, I thought about running after them, but then my bites started itching again and a girl was waving at us. The same girl who'd run out into the desert to get our ice creams. She was a bit older than us, and really tall. She smiled shyly, beckoning us over to a large muddy puddle.

And that's how I came to have my first ever mud bath. And I can tell you, it was *amazing*. After a morning of insane itching, the mud immediately made everything feel cooler. It was marvellous, magical, miracle mud.

I sat there, eyes shut, smiling, listening to the birds squawking in their cages, for about a minute.

MIRACLE MUD

And then Sadie Snickpick ruined everything.

'Girl,' she said, sounding like an empress, 'bring drinks.'

The girl looked nervous. And confused.

'Water.' Sadie raised her voice, and added a gesture with her hand. 'Now!'

I don't know what it is about Sadie. If I'd asked for that, the girl would have just ignored me. But when Sadie shouts people run.

'OK, come on. She's gone.'

'What?'

'We need to investigate.'

'I am investigating. Investigating the benefits of a miracle mud bath. The boy said we'd need three hours to suck all the poison out.'

'Don't be stupid. He just doesn't want us snooping around.'

'Why would—' I started, but she didn't let me finish.

'This is so dodgy. A ten-year-old from the future just happens to turn up at the exact same time and in the exact same place as us for a *school project*? And you think it's just a coincidence?'

Sadie gave me her look.

And she did have a point. Suddenly, sitting there in the mud bath, with the itching fading away, my mind started to work again. It *was* dodgy him being here, now, of all times and places.

My stomach lurched with a sudden flip of fear.

Johnnie and Myrt were out there alone with him.

'Don't tell me you don't want to find out what's going on up there.' Sadie pointed out into the desert, to the pyramid. Great clouds of smoke were billowing from the top of it. 'Your mum and dad have gotta be somewhere. The shoe, remember?'

She stood, looking about cautiously. Most of the Stone Agers had gone into the jungle with Johnnie to fetch the sofa. There were still a few around, but not many, and they were all busy carrying more pots of bird poo into the desert. A human conveyor belt up to the pyramid.

'Come on, before the girl comes back,' said Sadie, pulling herself out of the mud. Dripping everywhere, she ran to the nearest bird cage and forced it open. Before I could process what was going on, she'd managed to open a second. The third cage took longer, but she broke the knot with her big hands and soon had that open too. There were parrots everywhere, and then a sudden shouting from the desert.

She'd been spotted.

You can call me a wimp if you like, but I didn't even think about hanging around. I was up and out of that bath and running after Sadie, and together we disappeared into the jungle.

Diving for cover in the thick vegetation, we lay still, heads down. I struggled to get my breath back without making a noise, but I needn't have worried, because when I looked up no one was searching for us. They were too busy going nuts chasing after the birds.

'Right,' said Sadie, 'we go round the back of the pyramid and come up from behind.'

And that's what we did. Without another word and still covered in mud, she was off and running into the desert. And I ran after her, annoyed that I was just following, and struggling to keep up with her long, lollopy stride. We made our way round the back of the sand dune and then up. Until finally, after what felt like 10,000 steps, we reached the top.

But what we saw up there raised more questions than it answered. Because the pyramid was open and giving off the strangest smell.

I risked nearing the edge of the open hole and peered down into a giant chamber. It was like

something out of *Lord of the Rings* – row after row of massive smelting pots all filled with molten fires. Sweating children shovelled bird poo, feeding the fires.

How they stood the heat and the smell was beyond me. It kicked me in the nose like a bucket of mustard. Imagine a volcano that runs on poo for fuel. Now imagine the smell. Well, it was exactly like that.

'That's weird,' said Sadie Snickpick. She'd somehow got hold of Johnnie's telescope and was looking through it.

'What's weird?' I said, still struggling with the smell. 'This is exactly what he said we'd find. A factory for making gunpowder out of bird poo.'

'Not that, you idiot.' Sadie waved a dismissive hand at the pyramid. 'Look at *that*.'

She passed me the telescope, and pointed to the

back of the Sphinx. There was a hole in the ground at the base of the statue. And there, coiled up in the hot sun, was a giant snake. If the World's Ten Deadliest Snakes poster on Johnnie's bedroom wall was anything to go by, it was a rock python.

A big one.

'So what are you waiting for, Watson?' said Sadie. 'The game's afoot. No one uses a guard-snake unless they *really* don't want people snooping about.'

'Or maybe it's just having a nap in the sun?' I replied, wincing. But Sadie was right, this was one coincidence too many. There was something beneath the Sphinx that needed guarding. And it wasn't just ice cream.

'Heads or tails?' asked Sadie.

Without thinking, I answered, 'Heads?'

And, without another word, she pushed me head first down the side of the pyramid.

HOW TO SLIDE HEAD FIRST DOWN A GIANT SAND DUNE

I've since discovered that people actually do this for sport. But they use a board instead of their face.

By the time I got to the bottom, my face was sanded to a hot, raw pink. Sadie's shorts took a battering too, but tails was definitely the better option.

Her aim had been pretty amazing though, and with Sadie pulling on my arm we ran the last few metres to the Sphinx.

The python was gone. There were furrows in the sand where the snake had been lying, and a giant channel of sand headed down into the hole at the base of the giant statue. A channel wide enough to fit my leg.

I looked at the hole in the ground, a dark, narrow rectangle with steps leading down. And then I looked at Sadie.

'Don't look at me – I hate snakes,' she said, shaking her head. 'I hate 'em.'

I looked back into the hole. The first three steps were clear.

'Just stick your head in and take a look,' said Sadie.

I inched forward; the fourth step was empty too.

'Look, do you want to find your mum and dad or what?!' she said, giving me a verbal shove.

And then a blue-green parrot landed on the ground between us. It looked exhausted, like people had been chasing it all afternoon. (Which they probably had.)

Its wings were clipped to stop it flying very far, and I remember thinking, *How cruel.*

And then I heard shouting.

People were coming.

'Get down there, you idiot,' crackled Sadie's voice. 'We need to hide!'

HOW TO CRAWL INTO A SNAKE PIT

There's no *Book of Secrets* tip for this one. I mean, who needs to know that?

Except I needed to know. People were coming, I was desperate and, besides, we did need to find Mum and Dad.

So I basically made it up as I went along:

ELIZA'S GUIDE TO CRAWLING INTO A SNAKE PIT
(Do <u>NOT</u> try this at home[30])

Step 1: Close your eyes

Step 2: Cough nervously

Step 3: Try to remember that snakes are more scared of you than you are of them

---

30 In fact, don't try it anywhere

closed my eyes, but only for a few seconds, just so they would adjust to the dark. And then I coughed, so the snake wouldn't be surprised (most snakes just want to avoid you).

Now you're probably thinking, *Wow, Eliza is being weirdly super-brave. What's happened?* Well, the truth is, for some reason, I've never been *that* scared of big snakes. I mean the really big ones that eat pigs and horses. I've always thought: they're not poisonous, and they're so big and slow. You'd have to be pretty stupid to just sit there and let them squeeze you to death. And so, as I ducked my head down into the hole and saw that the first five steps were definitely clear, it didn't take a huge amount of bravery to start shuffling down on my bum with my eyes shut.

'Quickly!' whispered Sadie, quiet but angry.

I shuffled faster, one, two, four steps. Until my

head was inside the chamber and I could cough and look around. There was a low hum, like the sound of an old fridge, and a desk with stuff on it, and a hammock. And then I saw the python, curled up between two giant sarcophaguses at the entrance to a dark passageway.

Guardian of the Sarcophaguses

MYSTERY
SARCOPHAGUS #1

MYSTERY
SARCOPHAGUS #2

ARE THOSE EGGS??

IT'S GARGANTUAN

The snake's eyes were open, but it was breathing softly, like it was asleep. The closer I looked, the more convinced I was that it was coiled round a batch of giant eggs.

SNAkes Do Do thAt.

J x

This changed everything. There was no way she'd let us get anywhere near those. No mother would.

'It's got eggs,' I whispered up to Sadie. She was right behind me, squinting in the dark and gripping the blue-green parrot by the throat.

'They're close.' Her voice was so quiet, I barely heard it.

But I could hear people, footsteps in the sand, above our heads. They just had to look inside and we'd be caught.

Keeping one eye firmly on the snake, we inched over to the far wall and hid in the dark shadows, waiting.

Time goes slowly when you're hiding in a snake pit. I spent most of it watching the snake for signs of life. But it lay there, breathing softly up and down.

I don't remember when I first spotted the paintings. My pupils gradually got bigger until lines started appearing on the walls: first blacks and then yellows and reds. And suddenly the people above us, and Sadie and the parrot and even the python faded into the quiet of my mind. Because the more I looked, the clearer everything became. This ancient wall painting wasn't just a picture; it told a story.

No, I began to realize, it told a *history*.

A history that explained everything. Even the future.

Which, I guess, makes it a prophecy.

A prophecy with *me* in it.

It's probably best if I just draw it:

THE PROPHECY OF GIZA

'Look at the last picture.' said Sadie. 'Is that what happens next?'

'What? The End of the World?' I couldn't help asking out loud.

At that exact moment, as if it wanted to answer, the snake woke up.

The huge triangular head rose; the tongue tasted the air and, without any further warning, it slid towards us.

And, suddenly, I knew just how a rock python catches a pig.

HOW TO CATCH A PIG (IF YOU'RE A ROCK PYTHON)

The pig just freezes up in terror as the snake slowly slides towards it.

Luckily for me, I'm not as dumb as a pig.

'Get out!' I shouted, but Sadie was way ahead of me. She was halfway to the steps when the snake's tail tripped her up. She crashed down and the tail instinctively started to curl round her, but Sadie's quicker

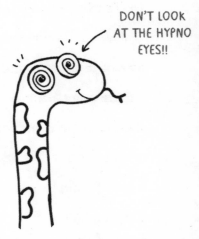

DON'T LOOK AT THE HYPNO EYES!!

ActuALLy, they usuALLy Drop DowN oN their prey from trees. if you're worrieD ABout rock pythoNs iN the juNgle, Look up, Not DowN.

J xx

than that, even scrabbling around in the dust.

Seeing Sadie scrambling for her life was the moment my brain burst. I ran, and got to the steps just behind her. My mind had stopped working and I grabbed her, dragging her back so I could push past. Desperate to do anything to get away from that snake.

I'm not proud of that, but it wasn't like I planned any of it. I just found myself pulling on Sadie's leg, tripping her up and clambering over her body to get out of that hideous snake pit. In that moment of pure terror, I'd have gladly dragged a thousand Sadie Snickpicks down into the path of those hideous fangs.

Sadie fought back, of course, kicking me in the chest. And for one horrible moment I thought I'd topple backwards right on to the python.

But I didn't.

Instead, as I struggled to keep my balance, a ball of blue-green feathers flashed past me. The feathers were almost black-grey in the dim light, and the parrot gave a surprised squawk as it shot by. It bounced on a step (and I remember thinking, *Birds bounce?*) and then another, and then finally into the open jaws of the rock python.

The python looked surprised. So did the parrot.

A rock python can dislocate its jaws and swallow an animal as big as a Labrador.

A parrot is more of a snack than a proper meal.

With its mouth full of parrot, the snake retreated. Sadie nodded at me, as if to say, 'We're safe now,' or maybe, 'Don't mess, or you're next,' or maybe just, 'Get off my leg!'

To be honest, I didn't have a clue what the nod meant. But, as she climbed back into daylight, I knew that, when push came to shove, Sadie Snickpick would shove me into the jaws of a rock python if it meant saving her own skin.

'They've gone,' she said, looking out into the bright day.

I'd forgotten all about the people. I crawled out on to the sand, a picture of Greeny in my head.[31]

'We have to go,' said Sadie. Her hands were shaking, and I realized mine weren't. That somehow made me feel better, calmer.

---

31 It was only after we heard the last of its bones cracking that I realized I'd given Greeny a name in my head.

We left without looking back. Left the chamber with its secrets and prophecies, wanting never to go down there again. Never in a billion years.

But as we ran, circling out and back into the rainforest, I knew in my head that I had no choice. The Riddle of the Sphinx couldn't stay unsolved for ever, because if it did I'd never see Mum and Dad again. That wall painting down there didn't just tell a story. It told *my* story. And, if it was ever going to have a better ending (than the *End of the World*), then I had to go back: get past the python, and find Mum and Dad. But first we needed weapons, and a plan. Johnnie would have a plan.

We finally worked our way through the jungle back to the mud bath. If anyone noticed we'd been missing, they didn't say anything; they were still too busy catching parrots. I soon realized, as I sat there up to my neck in a giant muddy puddle, that the Stone Agers weren't just worried. They were afraid. There was proper fear on their faces as they struggled to get the birds back in their cages.

I thought back to the wall painting.

They were frightened of the boy. Of their god.

Their god, who was out in the rainforest with my baby brother.

And then, without any more time to worry than that, there was shouting and running about. Because riding into the camp, carried on our new brown sofa and shouting instructions like a roman emperor, was Johnnie.

And he had the biggest smile you've ever seen.

HOW TO WIPE THE SMILE OFF YOUR BROTHER'S FACE

Myrt, it turned out, had found the sofa pretty much immediately. Her nose and the path of smashed trees meant they'd been able to find it quickly. It was only about five miles away, after all. And then, a bit of straining and machete-hacking later, they'd got back. Johnnie and Myrt had overseen the whole thing from their seats on the sofa.

He seemed to think we'd be full of praise and gratitude for him sitting on his butt all afternoon, but both Sadie and I only had eyes for *the boy*. And the boy was completely focused on the sofa, shouting at everyone as if he thought it might be bumped, or dropped. The more we watched, the more I saw we'd been right.

They *were* afraid of him.

He barely spoke to us, so busy was he to get the sofa under cover, shouting orders for a lean-to shelter to be erected out of ferns and jungle leaves. And it was a good job he did, because it then began to rain. A deluge, as my dad would have called it. With huge, heavy drops so big you could tell when each one hit your face.

It rained and we ran, back to the treehouse that was now our home. Up there I sat, wet, weary and worried, looking out into the desert as the black clouds churned up the sand in great splodges.

Johnnie was full of chat, babbling on about how clever he'd been, finding the sofa. Cuddling Myrt like they'd both come back from some epic quest.

'Johnnie,' I said eventually. 'Has it ever occurred to you that you've just given away our only hope of getting back to the future?'

Johnnie's smile disappeared in an instant.

'What d'you mean?'

'I mean, Johnnie, that this boy isn't our friend. He's the enemy.'

We told Johnnie everything then, about the chamber beneath the Sphinx, about the snake guarding the passageways beyond, and the mysterious sarcophaguses. But, most of all, we told him about the wall painting.

'Mum and Dad were on there, Johnst, fighting the boy, but years ago.'

'But how? He's only ten.' Johnnie immediately answered his own question. 'Time travel?!'

'What I wanna know,' said Sadie, interrupting, 'is why he's hanging around. Why's he still here? If he's got a time machine, why not go back to where he came from?'

'Maybe his time machine really is broken,' said Johnnie.

'Or maybe he's been waiting for us,' I said suddenly. As soon as I said it, I knew it was true. 'He's been waiting for us! This is all one enormous trap, and we've fallen right into it.'

Johnnie was getting agitated, which was bad. Sadie looked thoughtful, and somehow that was worse.

'But why?' said Johnnie eventually.

'That's not the question.'

We both turned to Sadie; her eyes were black in the early evening light.

'The question is, *who* is he?'

The silence hung over us.

We didn't even know his name.

'He says they don't have names in the future just—'

'You believe that rubbish?'

Now Sadie said it out loud, it did seem a bit ridiculous. Johnnie obviously realized the same thing, because his mouth stayed open, but nothing came out.

'So, come on, who is he?' Sadie said it more like a threat than a question. And it sat in the air for a bit.

'Well, at least we know it can't be Noah – the boy's about thirty years too young. You don't think Noah had a son, do you?' said Johnnie, and the thought made my stomach lurch.

But it just wasn't possible.

'He's the wrong age. No one's worn jeans like those since before we were born. Trust me, Johnst, I know more about fashion than you ever will, and the boy is definitely *not* Noah's son.'

'Maybe he's the Time Police,' said Johnnie, his eyes opening wider.

Sadie snorted, so Johnnie explained.

'In every time-travel movie, once humans invent time travel, they have to invent Time Police.'

'Why?' Sadie didn't look convinced.

'Because baddies try to go back in time and change the timeline and take over the world. Obviously.'

'So you're saying he's trying to stop us because *we're* the baddies?' said Sadie.

That shut Johnnie up.

'There is *something* we know,' I said, and three faces turned to me – even Myrt looked up. 'The final picture on the wall. The volcano. The prophecy picture. I think he's trying to kill every human on the planet.'

'Don't be silly,' said Johnnie. 'He'd need a nuclear bomb for that.'

But suddenly Johnnie's eyes went big and he started scrambling in his rucksack for a pencil.

would be a good thing. Maybe the planet was better off without us.

And then I had a terrible thought.

'Johnnie, if everyone's destroyed by a giant man-made volcano before we're born, does that mean we stop existing?'

Johnnie just shrugged and pulled his potato face.→

One thing was certain: this was bad. And, if we were going to save everyone on the planet, we needed the mother of all cunning plans.

HOW TO COME UP WITH THE MOTHER OF ALL CUNNING PLANS

For the rest of the evening, with the rain hammering down on our flimsy little treehouse roof, we argued.

A lot.

Everyone had a different idea about what to do next. Sadie paced around like a caged animal. She just wanted to attack the boy, attack everybody, everything.

Johnnie wanted to make a new controller for the sofa and get a billion miles away. Myrt was happy just curled up on my lap.

And me?

Well, I wanted to find Mum and Dad. I thought back to the wall painting. In that fourth picture, Mum and Dad were *underneath* the Sphinx.

'Johnnie, gimme Dad's shoe.'

I grabbed his rucksack impatiently, pulled out Dad's shoe and studied the picture.

'Look at the arrow.'

Sadie snatched the shoe. 'What about it?'

'I think we need to go *beneath* the Sphinx. The Riddle of the Sphinx, that open doorway . . . I think it's the only way we're going to find Mum and Dad.'

'What does "Myrtle follow myrtle!" mean?' asked Sadie, reading the words circled in thick pen.

We all looked at Myrt, but she was busy chewing her back leg.

Sadie argued for a while after that. And Johnnie shook his head a lot. The argument went round in circles until, finally, I grabbed Johnnie's hands.

'Johnnie, we can't run away – think of Mum and Dad.' I squeezed his hand three times, like Dad does when he wants to say 'I love you', and suddenly Johnnie's eyes filled with tears.

'OK,' he said simply, 'I'll go with you.'

'No, Johnnie, it's too dangerous. And the stairs are really steep.'

'I'm coming with you, 'Liza.' He squeezed my hand back, and now it was my turn to feel tears welling up.

'Besides,' he said, suddenly brightening, 'it's not

like we need to worry about the snake.'

That got Sadie's attention. 'Why not, little man?'

Johnnie smiled. 'Because a snake with a bellyful of parrot on a cold desert night isn't doing much.'

Sadie looked at me as if to say, 'Are we gonna take a five-year-old's word for it?'

'Johnnie's read Google,' I said simply.

'And, if the snake does move, we can always charm it.'

'This is insane,' said Sadie. 'We've got weapons; we can just go down and kill it.'

'What weapons?!' Johnnie looked theatrically round the treehouse to make his point.

Sadie threw a banana into his face to make hers.

'Numb-nut. Anything can be a weapon if you know how to use it.' She looked about too, her gaze finally resting on my hair. 'Even Eliza's hair bobble can be a weapon.'

Johnnie went quiet after that. I could see he wanted to say, 'How can a hair bobble be a weapon?' but was too afraid to ask.

In fact, we were all quiet for a bit. The rain fell and we ate bananas while Johnnie flicked through *The Book of Secrets*.

Eventually, he began to read out loud:

SECRET 91: HOW TO CHARM A SNAKE

Everybody knows that snake charming is just a myth, and if you try it for real then you'll get dead.

BUT Secret 91 is this:

Charming a snake is EASY: you just need a cold, well-fed snake and for it to be dark. And you'll also need a bright light. Oh, and you'll definitely need nerves of steel and antivenom (in case it goes horribly, agonizingly wrong).

Step 1: cover the light, and then

Step 2: uncover the light.

Step 3: Repeat (and this is the crucial bit): Do it in time with the snake's breathing.

Snake breathes in: cover the light.
Snake breathes out: uncover.

Step 4: There is no step 4.
Tick as appropriate:

☐ Check me out! I've just charmed a snake

or

☐ I'm dead.

PS If you try this on a rock python or boa constrictor, bring a pair of scissors in case you have to cut your way out.

See also *Secret 101: How to Run With a Pair of Scissors.*

I read with a sinking heart. *The Book of Secrets* hardly ever puts warnings in like that. Even **Secret 84: How to Ride an Ostrich** only has one warning.[32] This had *two*.

Sadie read over my shoulder and muttered something like, 'This is insane.'

I looked back at the book, and then at Johnnie.

'What do you think, Johnst?'

'I think we should all go. But let's wait a bit.'

He was right; the rain was louder than ever. Besides, we'd be better off waiting till everyone was asleep.

As the old saying goes: when the going gets tough, the tough catch a bit of shut-eye.

---

32 Warning: when you fall off, try not to fall off the back. A kick from an ostrich can kill a lion.

HOW TO CATCH A
BIT OF SHUT-EYE

I couldn't sleep.

Sadie Snickpick snores, for one thing. And she had the mattress, leaving me and Johnnie and Myrt to share the hammock. That was never gonna work. The other thing was the singing Sphinx.

Johnnie had warned me about this, but it didn't make it any easier to ignore. The rain had gone, but an evening breeze from the cooling desert blew over the dunes, making a low background hum. Then, as the wind picked up, it whistled and wailed as it blew round the Sphinx's head and neck. The statue sounded like an injured animal, crying to be put out of its misery. No wonder everyone thinks the Sphinx is haunted.

And so, without waiting for the sky to turn completely black, I climbed out of the hammock and tiptoed over to the door of our treehouse. The clouds were clearing and the stars were coming out brightly. I could see the Sphinx properly now the storm had passed, and the pyramid too. Behind me, I heard jungle sounds: monkeys hunting at night, birds restless in their cages, and the humming, clicking buzz of a billion insects.

Then I looked down, and the warning lights in my brain went ballistic. The rope basket, our only way down, had gone.

'Johnnie!' I whispered, shaking him awake. 'They've taken the rope lift. We're trapped.'

Johnnie's eyes were blurry, but they were open, and I could see them trying to focus in the dark.

'We're trapped.'

Sadie was awake now too, and her brain was quicker to understand the situation.

'He's on to us,' she said, squinting over the side. 'We need to find your mum and dad right now.'

She immediately started untying the hammock. 'I'll lower you halfway; you can jump the rest.'

'You want me to get in that?' I said.

'Well, you're not strong enough to lower me, and Johnnie's a wuss.'

I looked at Johnnie and he just shrugged.

'When you get down there, find some rope and toss it up,' she said, untying the hammock.

'I'll break my legs.'

'It's sand, you wimp. You can't break anything on sand. Now get in and stop arguing.'

I looked at Johnnie, and at Myrt, and I knew I had no choice. This was going to take a leap into the dark.

HOW TO JUMP OUT
OF A TREE

'The secret is, don't try to fight gravity. Just relax,' said Johnnie, with zero helpfulness.

I was hanging, gripping on to the string hammock, not even halfway down the tree. I couldn't even remember what the ground looked like.

'Just jump!' whispered Sadie.

But I couldn't do it.

'I can't!' I whispered back.

Then she let go. And I crashed to the ground.

How I didn't break both ankles is a mystery. And how I managed not to scream is an even bigger one. I just slammed into the sand and the air came smashing out of me so fast I didn't even get to call

Sadie a really bad name.

By the time I did get my breath back, I was just glad no one had seen me. I looked around for the rope ladder, or anything. But there was nothing I could use. And Johnnie's whisper was enough to wake the dead.

'Is the ladder down there?'

'Shut up, Johnnie,' I whispered back. 'I'm looking.'

Then his rucksack landed on me

'Johnnie? You almost killed me.'

And then Myrt landed on me, and almost killed me.

She'd jumped, assuming I'd catch her. Not realizing I couldn't even see her in the dark. Stupid dog. But I didn't have so much as a second to tell her off before she was up and running.

Straight into the desert.

Stupid dog.

I looked up to see Sadie and Johnnie. Two faces peering down at me through the gloom.

'There's nothing here!' I whispered loudly. Myrt started barking, out in the desert beyond where I could see.

'I've gotta go. There's no rope, no ladder, no nothing.'[33]

And, before Johnnie could point out my double negative, I ran into the desert after Myrt.

Her bark took me right towards the Sphinx, like it was my destiny to go there that night. My destiny to Solve the Riddle of the Sphinx's Butt.

I ran fast and it didn't take long to find her. She'd

---

33 Johnnie, I know this is a double negative. Please don't correct it. It's a record of what I actually said. Normal people use double negatives all the time. Especially when they've just almost broken both legs and have to go rescue their dog from the middle of a snake-filled desert. In fact, Johnnie, just stop making corrections to *my* journal. Write your own journal. THIS IS MINE!

stopped barking (thank God) but was scampering about in circles at the back of the Sphinx. She goes crazy when she's out at night, especially after a hot day, and she was like that now, ears back, eyes wild, zigging about with a nose full of smells. But always going back to the hole at the back of the Sphinx.

I'd kind of half expected there to be guards or something, but there wasn't anything. Nothing that I could see anyway. I hid with my back to the stone, praying that Myrt wouldn't start barking again.

The sands were shifting with a low groan, then the breeze picked up again and the desert started its humming. Louder and louder until it rumbled into a thrum that hit you in the chest. And, suddenly, I felt proper fear. Myrt and I were alone, in a different time, and surrounded by people who wanted us dead.

As more clouds gathered overhead and more stars

disappeared, the wind grew stronger. This time, as it rushed over and round the stone Sphinx, the howling reached a scream. It was like the lion itself was screaming, screaming a warning.

Or maybe it screamed because it knew I was about to uncover its secret.

I edged my way along the side of the giant statue, past its back leg and finally to its tail. I thought of Johnnie saying, 'We've gotta get into its butt' and, despite everything, it almost made me smile. But Myrt was at the opening, and she was about to start barking again.

'Heel, Myrt, to heel!' I whispered, but Myrt never did understand any of her commands. She went straight down, right into the black hole. As if she was too stupid to be afraid of snakes. Which she was.

I stood there, paralysed at the thought of that

massive reptile – and maybe worse.

But with more clouds filling the night sky, and stars blinking out fast, I knew it was now or never. It was time to swallow down my fear, and trust that Johnnie was right about snakes with full bellies on cold nights.

It was time to solve the Riddle of the Sphinx's Butt.

HOW TO SOLVE THE RIDDLE
OF THE SPHINX'S BUTT

If life's a horror movie,[34] then this would be the part where everyone in the audience screams, 'Go back, Eliza, you IDIOT!'

---

34 And there's a really good chance it is.

But sometimes in life, just like in films, you have to be an idiot to get anywhere. If Mum and Dad were trapped down there, then I had to get them. Besides, Myrt had let out another bark. And when she barks it's loud enough to wake the dead, let alone a sleeping snake. I imagined Myrt being crushed by the python and found myself creeping into the chamber, bumping down the steps on my backside. In the dark, the ceiling felt horribly, *crushingly*, low.

And, as I went down, the last of the starlight faded away to total blackness.

I reached the bottom, feeling around blindly with my foot to make sure it was OK to stand, terrified of brushing against the snake. Myrt squirmed against me, and I carefully got to my feet.

We were in the bowels of the Sphinx.

I gripped Myrt's collar and listened. Listened

for the snake, wondering if I'd hear it sliding towards us across the stone floor.

For what felt like ages, I listened.

But I couldn't hear anything.

It was time to risk using Johnnie's torch. The light was feeble, but as soon as I dropped it into the water bottle from the rucksack it instantly lit up the room.

I immediately felt like I was in the middle of one of my cousin Oscar's horrendo computer games. You know the type, where you're constantly having to make decisions and look everywhere and you're always lost, and then just when you figure out where to go someone jumps out and whaps you round the head.

You probably love 'em.

In real life: not so fun. Especially when your only weapon is a hair bobble.

The snake was coiled up in a corner, eyes open, but asleep. I could see its parrot-fed belly moving softly up and down. Johnnie was right about that bit at least. But I knew now how fast it could move when it did wake, and my heart didn't slow a beat.

Now what? I thought.

What would *you* do?

My best weapon was an elastic hair bobble, and I only had one life. Would you open Mystery Sarcophagus #1? Or Mystery Sarcophagus #2? Jump over the snake and push on into the dark passageway? Search the table? The hammock? Translate the hieroglyphs?? Kill the snake while it slept? (With a hair bobble???!) Run for your life?

Not easy, huh?

I looked about, desperation rising in my stomach. The whole thing screamed:

!!DANGER!!
!!LEVEL BADDiE!!
!!APPROACHiNG!!

I knew that what I did next was going to seriously matter, in a way that not many things you do actually matter.

So what *would* you have done?

The first thing *I* did was get an ice lolly.

I didn't mean to. I crept over to Mystery Sarcophagus #1 and pulled on the giant lever. The heavy door swung open, blasting me with cold air. Inside, it was neatly stacked with shelf after shelf of ice creams and ice lollies. It was just a freezer.

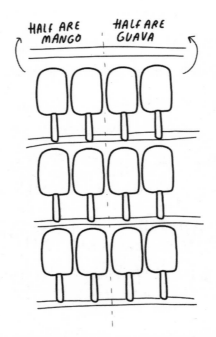

The second thing I did was choose mango, because guava always tastes a bit funny. Think it's crazy to start ice-lollying in the middle of a mystery-busting break-in? Well, you're wrong. A cool, rehydrated head thinks twenty-five per cent faster.[35] And, besides, it was a free ice lolly.

The third thing I did was open the other sarcophagus, Mystery Sarcophagus #2. And *that* was the thing that mattered.

That was the thing that changed my life.

For ever.

My spidey senses were screaming as I pulled back the giant lever. I just knew that whatever was inside was going to explain everything.

Again, the stone door swung open under its own

---

35 It's true, see *The Book of Secrets*, **Secret 28: How to Ace your SATS**. You wanna pass your SATS on a hot day? Stick a home-made ice lolly in your pencil case. (Cheat Code: write answers on the stick!)

massive weight. And my heart literally jumped in my chest.

It was another freezer, all right. But there were no lollies in this one. What I saw inside Mystery Sarcophagus #2 was the most hideous thing anyone has ever seen.

I looked at it for about three seconds.

And then my brain collapsed.

HOW TO RECOVER FROM A COLLAPSED BRAIN

Sure, some basic functions kept going. I didn't just fall down dead. But, apart from the bits of brain that keep you standing up and breathing and tell your bum to stay shut,[36] everything else closed down. Even the bit of brain that keeps your mouth from flopping open.

MOUTH = OPEN

BUM = SHUT

---

36 Does it work like that?? Does your brain have to constantly tell your bum to 'hold it!'? Or does your bum just assume 'hold tight until brain tells me to do something different'? That would make more sense, but who knows? Let's hope we never find out.

Because right here, trapped inside Mystery Sarcophagus #2, with icy vapour clouds swirling around him, was Dad.

My dad.

Turned into an ice statue.

MOUTH STILL FLOPPY

He looked like he was reaching out in agony, and for a moment I imagined the pain he must have felt at being frozen to death. But then I recognized the look on his face. It was the look Dad has when he's reaching for the last biscuit.

I leaned forward to touch his face and immediately my fingertips burned with cold.

'I wouldn't defrost him just yet,' said a voice behind me, and my brain fired back into life.

'It gets real messy. And you'll definitely want a doctor handy.' I suddenly recognized the voice, recognized it from 7,053 years in the future.

I spun to see Boy-God sitting up in the hammock.[37] He had some sort of laser gun in his hand. Maybe it was his voice, the way he said the words 'real messy', but, as he swung his feet on to the floor and wiped clean his glasses, I suddenly knew *exactly* who he was.

'Noah?' I said quietly.

'Yip, that's me.'

'But . . . you're a middle-aged man?' I looked at his trainers. 'You're way too old for those.'

---

37 If you'd gone for option 'search the hammock', then well done you. But *you* didn't get an ice lolly and it's too late now.

'I'm not even eleven, ya dumb-nut.'

Without his glasses on, it was all so obvious.

One eye was bigger than the other. Why hadn't

 I noticed that before? Why hadn't *Johnnie* noticed?

'But . . .' I said, my brain spinning.

'But how did I get here aged ten years and nine months?'

I nodded, still dazed.

'This is my first trip; I invented my time machine when I was ten. Before I met you. In 2053.' He held something in his hand, and in the dim light it took me a while to realize what it was. It was a battered old wodge of paper inside a big bulldog clip, but I recognized it immediately. It was a photocopy of my old journal. Dad had wanted to read it the day before he disappeared.

'How did you get that?' I shouted, but he just laughed.

'And how can you be here *and* in the future?' My brain was exploding back to full size, struggling to take all this in. 'You can't be a grown-up and a kid at the same time.'

The boy smiled.

'Yes, I can; I'm a clone, just like you. Except I wasn't stupid enough to obliterate the original.'

'So you're just a copy? But what about the negative . . .' I wanted to say 'energy' but couldn't quite remember if that was the right word.

'The negative energy?'

I nodded.

'You sacrifice something else. A small cow or a big pig. Anything the same size. Only an idiot like your father wouldn't think of that.'

This boy was a monster. I turned to Dad, all my anger flooding back. 'What have you done to him?'

The boy, I still couldn't think of him as Noah, walked over and knocked his knuckles on Dad's chest.

I wanted to punch him for doing that, but he never once lowered the gun. So I just stood there, frozen and useless like my dad.

'He's frozen in carbonite. Don't worry, it's perfectly safe. He could stay like that for ever. As long as no one accidentally pulls the plug.' He shut the freezer door with a fake frown, as if to say, 'Don't waste electricity, young lady – it's bad for the environment.'

'But why?'

'Let's just say I need to kill him, but not just yet.

He's insurance, you see.'

'Insurance?'

'Against your mum. She won't dare do anything, knowing it would put her beloved hubby in danger. She's still down there, you know.' He nodded towards the dark passageway. 'It's like a maze; the passages go on for ever. But she won't risk anything as long as she knows I can pull the plug on yer dad. Or maybe she's lost, just like everybody I've ever sent down to find her.'

At that moment – Dad frozen, Mum in hiding, Noah's big eye grinning at me through his dorky glasses – any lingering hope drained out of me.

Myrt growled, and I grabbed her before she got herself shot.

I thought about Johnnie, but he couldn't help. He couldn't even get out of the treehouse.

And Sadie was only out for herself.

Everything was down to me, and there was nothing I could do. Not alone. Not with a laser gun in my face.

Like Johnnie said, I was just a little drip in a massive ocean.

I squeezed my fist, and felt my fingernails biting into the palm of my hand.

Everything was lost.

And then, who knows how, my brain imagined exactly what I needed to do. Imagined *precisely* how to beat a Level Baddie-with-a-Laser-Gun. It was like a video game playing out in my head:

HOW TO FIGHT A LEVEL BADDIE
(WITH A LASER GUN) USING A HAIR BOBBLE

That's how it worked in my head. Unfortunately,

in reality:

HOW NOT TO FIGHT A LEVEL BADDIE
(WITH A LASER GUN)

So I chewed his tutti-frutti[38] bubblegum and listened as the Boy-Noah leant himself against the wall and laughed.

'It's nothing personal. I just need to kill your entire family, because the Lemon family are the only people who can stop me.'

'Stop you doing what?'

'Cleaning up the planet, of course. You Lemons have all got time machines, and I can't leave any loose ends. Not with you lot running wild in space-time.'

'Cleaning up the planet? You mean *destroying* it.'

'I'm not destroying the planet, you gump. I'm *curing* it. Humans are a disease. A germ that doesn't know when to stop multiplying. We double and double and double until we choke it to death.'

I pulled a face. 'And you think killing everybody will help?'

---

38 What is tutti-frutti anyway?

'I *know* it will help.'

'Why do you hate humans so much?'

'Because I know what happens, Eliza Lemon. I've been there, to the future. I've been everywhere. I know what *happens at the end*.'

I stopped talking then. I obviously wanted to ask him, 'What does happen at the end?' but I didn't. The gleam in his eye stopped me; maybe learning about the future had driven him mad.

'Do you know how many times I've tried to stop human beings destroying the planet? Do you?' He snorted. 'Human beings, such a ridiculous term. If humans would only just "be" . . . "Be" happy, "be" satisfied with what they've got, there wouldn't be a problem. But they're not human *be*ings, are they, Eliza? They're human takings, human snatchings, human shoppings.'

He was properly ranting now. I kind of knew

what he was trying to say, but it was a bit over the top. Especially coming from a ten-year-old.

Besides, at that exact moment, Sadie Snickpick came to the rescue.

She was creeping down the steps, and in the shadow of my little bottle-light I could see she had a weapon. My eyes almost popped when I saw her, and I grabbed on to Myrt to stop her from barking, but Boy-Noah was too busy with his lecture to notice.

Sadie steadily crept down, weapon aloft, just long enough for me to see what it was.

My heart sank. It was Johnnie's Brussels sprout stalk.

And then my disappointment doubled, because Sadie Snickpick tripped, fell and landed right on the floor between Noah and me.

I glared at her and said the first words that fell into my mouth.

'What are you doing?'

'What's it look like?' she said, angry as ever. 'It's a rescue, idiot.'

I looked up at the gun in Noah's hand, and then back at Sadie, sprawled on the floor.

'With sprouts??'

She didn't need to answer, her face said it all, but she did anyway:

'Obviously.'

HOW TO RESCUE SOMEONE WITH SPROUTS

You have to give it to Sadie: she moved like a dancer. I could almost hear the music as she slid left, spun right and then launched herself in a totally random direction. Noah fired his gun, but the pulse of red light missed Sadie completely, biting into the stone floor with a cloud of dust and rock.

Lasers in a jungle! I remember thinking, half remembering the words to a song my dad used to sing.

Sadie was so fast, Noah couldn't get near her. Suddenly a sprout flicked out of her left hand, then another and another. Like poison darts they fizzed through the air, smacking again and again into Noah's face. His glasses flew up and, before he could fire again, Sadie was jamming the stalk into his face.

HOW TO 'GET SOMEONE' WITH SPROUTS

GLASSES ARE FLYING OFF HIS HEAD

GETTING THE 70-DEGREE ANGLE IS CRITICAL: THE NOSE EITHER GOES INTO THE BRAIN OR THE HEAD TIPS BACK

He fell backwards, and I heard a crack as his head hit the floor. But Noah Junior held on to the gun, and now he started firing blindly. Beams of light shot everywhere, kicking off the walls and throwing up great chunks of rock. Myrt went wild – she almost squirmed out of her collar, but I held on tight.

And finally, inevitably, the laser hit the sleeping rock python, right on the back of its head.

It reared up like an electric shock, and lunged forward in a blind attack.

'Run!' shouted Sadie, dodging the snake.

She didn't need to say it twice.

With Myrt at my heels, I ran right past her, straight into the black passageway.

I ran into the dark, and I ran for my life.

HOW TO RUN FOR YOUR LIFE

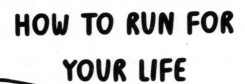

Secret 139: How to Run
For Your Life
Fast and zigzaggy.

That's what it tells you to do in *The Book of Secrets*.

I tried it.

And smashed into a wall.

Sadie yanked me to my feet and dragged me further into the darkness. We ran together like that, holding hands, Myrt under our feet, for what seemed like ages. Into a maze of corridors, none of them lit, getting darker and darker, until finally Sadie stopped.

I tried to say something, but she clamped a hand over my mouth. It smelled of sprouts.

'Shut up!' she hissed.

We waited for what seemed like ages. Until, finally, Sadie took her Brusselly hand off my face.

'Where are we?' I asked.

'How should I know?'

I looked around, but it was so dark I couldn't see anything. I held up my hand, right in front of my face, but I couldn't even see that. It was like my hand wasn't there. And, without thinking, I slapped myself, just to make sure it hadn't come off.

'What are you doing?' whispered Sadie.

'I don't know,' I said honestly, and looked around, even though it was pointless.

Look at this with your eyes shut. That's how

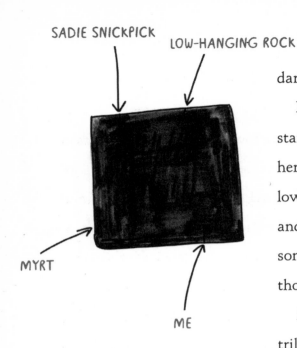

SADIE SNICKPICK   LOW-HANGING ROCK

MYRT

ME

dark it was.

I heard Sadie stand up and bang her head on a low-hanging rock, and then I heard something I never thought I'd hear.

Not in a trillion, trillion lifetimes.

I heard Sadie Snickpick have a panic attack.

'Are you OK?'

I just didn't know what else to say. Sadie Snickpick crying?? It was like a dolphin riding a golf buggy or a shoe singing Christmas carols.

She reached out for my hand and gripped it. This was beyond weird.

'I don't like small spaces.' I could feel her hesitate

and then she added, 'Not in the dark.'

My brain went off like a fire cracker. Sadie Snickpick was scared of the dark? I felt some sort of energy pulse through me, filling my arms and legs. Like I was growing bigger, stronger. I had to stand up I felt so fidgety.

I immediately smacked my head on the same thing Sadie had smacked hers on. But even that didn't dent my new-found confidence. Sadie Snickpick was afraid of the dark. Say it again and say it loud, Sadie-the-Sadist Snickpick, the biggest bully in the known universe, **was afraid of the dark**.

But then I heard a voice ringing through the darkness. It came thundering towards us from every direction.

And, suddenly, I was afraid of the dark too.

WHAT TO DO WHEN YOU'RE AFRAID OF THE DARK

'Come back, Eliza.'

The voice bellowed down the tunnel like a whole choir of voices. The word 'echo' doesn't even come close to describing it. It was like the voice had split through a hundred tunnels, rebounding around and around in the dark until one after the other they smacked into my ears.

Noah's voice sounded like the **Voice of God** from an old film, far away and close all at the same time.

I felt Sadie's grip tighten.

'I know you can you hear me. D'you understand the riddle now? The Riddle of the Sphinx? I mean, do you really understand?'

The echoing voices faded to silence. Sadie's hand was wet with sweat.

'The labyrinth's kept the secret safe for thousands of years. No one's ever come out. It's a labyrinth of d—'

I never heard the last word because Sadie finally broke out into a gasping sob.

'Shush,' I said, irritated. 'Did he say labyrinth of doom or labyrinth of death?' But Sadie was beyond answering.

'When I get to zero, I'm sending the python down, Eliza. So it can sniff out its next meal.'

I immediately imagined that snake tongue, tasting fear and Brussels sprouts on the wet underground air. I imagined it sliding up to us in the dark, wrapping itself round our legs so we couldn't move.

I wanted to scream, but Sadie's nails dug harder into my hand and the pain jolted me into silence.

'Do you want to be its next meal, Eliza?'

There was a pause.

'I'll cut you a deal – come out now and I won't sacrifice Johnnie to the volcano.'

Johnnie! We'd left him all alone . . . again!! And this time he didn't even have Myrt. But Noah wouldn't stop talking, and my brain couldn't keep up.

'Let me save you, Eliza. Bring your friend and follow my voice.' There was another pause before Noah continued. 'It's the only way out. Trust me on that. Unless you want to become snake poo in the dark, **follow my voice**.'

Sadie's grip was so tight my hand had gone numb. Myrt barked into the darkness.

'We *have* to do what he says,' she said, and I barely

recognized her voice, it sounded so full of fear.

'We can't,' I said. 'We have to find our own way out.' But I knew it was hopeless. Even if I hadn't dropped the torch, it would be hopeless. The labyrinth had been designed to keep its secrets.

'No one ever comes out, Eliza. Not without help,' the voice came again. 'I'll count, to give you time. Follow my voice and pray I don't get to zero. Fifty, forty-nine, forty-eight . . .'

I was stuck in a labyrinth of death/doom with a vicious bully who'd turned into a jelly baby, and the only way out was to follow the voice of a laser-wielding, ten-year-old maniac.

This was bad.

HOW TO ESCAPE FROM A LABYRINTH OF DEATH/DOOM

'Thirty-four, thirty-three . . .'

What would Johnnie do? I remember thinking, but it didn't help. He'd just hide and cuddle Myrt. She pressed against my legs in the dark, and I could hear her sniffing, like she always does at night.

Without really thinking, I found myself copying her, sniffing the air to see what she could smell. I sniffed in a great chest full of damp underground air. It was rich with Sadie's sprouts, but I was sure there was something else, something hidden behind it. Some other smell that made me think of home. I felt Myrt's head bob up, right against my knee.

She'd smelled something, I was sure of it. 'Myrt's the magnet.' Johnnie had said this morning at lunch. 'She can find anything.'

Myrtle follow myrtle!

And suddenly Dad's shoe made more sense.

Myrt could sniff out Mum through a thousand labyrinths.

'Myrty,' I said, struggling to keep the excitement out of my voice, 'go find her.'

Myrt's eyes blinked up at me in the dark, and then she was gone, sprinting away with a clatter of paws on the floor.

When I realized what I'd done, the smile dropped off my face.

'Myrt!' I shouted, and we started after her, but it was useless.

'Stupid dog,' said Sadie. 'Now what?'

'Two, one . . .'

Noah's countdown chuntered down to zero and, with the sound of Myrt's paws fading to nothing, I knew that we didn't have much choice. There was a snake on the loose. If we were going to sniff our way out of the labyrinth of doom/death, we were gonna have to do it without the dog.

HOW TO ESCAPE A LABYRINTH OF DEATH/ DOOM WITHOUT THE DOG

'Sadie, we've got to get away from these sprouts,' I said, forming a plan in my head. The smell of sprouts was just getting stronger and stronger. I prised the weapon out of her hand and tossed it away.

Holding hands in the dark, we walked slowly in the direction we'd heard Myrt run, crouched low to avoid the rocky ceiling. Deeper into the labyrinth we went, or maybe less deep. Who knew? Without Noah's voice, it was impossible to tell.

As we walked, I found myself sniffing the air, wondering at Myrt's sense of smell. Until finally we came to a split in the passageway.

'Now what?' asked Sadie, panic returning to her voice.

'Myrty?' I cried out, but the word just echoed back at me.

I sniffed again.

'Stop it; you're not a dog. You can't *sniff* your way out.'

But I *could* smell something.

'Be quiet,' I whispered, and gripped her hand tightly to make the point. There was something on the edge of my brain, a smell that I knew was somehow important.

Sniffing like that, in the dark and in total silence, it was like all my other senses were fading away. Leaving just the one. My sense of smell.

I took another sniff. And this time I was sure there was something.

The faintest of smells, but unmistakable. Unmistakable because I'd smelled it every day of my life.

It was the smell of myrtle. Not the dog – she smells like a wet sock. It was myrtle the *herb*. My mum's *favourite* herb. The sweet, fresh, herby green smell of the myrtle bush that's been growing outside our kitchen door since before I was born.

Suddenly the words on Dad's old shoe made total sense.

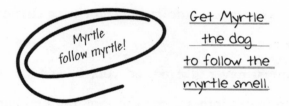

Myrtle follow myrtle!

Get Myrtle
the dog
to follow the
myrtle smell.

'Can't you smell that?' I asked, worried that I was imagining it.

I heard Sadie blowing hard and sucking snot. Heard a sleeve wipe across her face, and then the unmistakable sound of her sucking in air.

'Smell what?' she said after a few seconds.

'It's a plant, a herb. It smells a bit like rosemary and sage and bay all mixed up together. We need to follow it.'

'Are you out of your mind?'

'Come on, Sadie, we can't just give up. You have to trust me.'

I don't know if it was what I said, or perhaps it was just the very real threat of a rock python making its way towards us, but something changed between us.

'You just never give up, do you, Eliza Lemon?' And without another word she took my hand and let me lead her further into the labyrinth.

We walked together, still holding hands, and soon came to a fork in the passage.

The smell was definitely getting stronger.

Or was it?

I sniffed again and suddenly I couldn't smell it at all. It was like I'd just imagined everything.

'We go left,' I said with a confidence I didn't feel.

And that's how we made our first choice. Our first step towards freedom. And, in life, the first step is always the hardest.

Step by step, choice by choice, we made our way through the maze of tunnels. Always following where the smell of myrtle was strongest. Sometimes the smell faded and we had to retrace our steps, but we never gave up.

I never gave up.

After a long time, it got easier. Until even Sadie could smell it, and then, finally, I realized I could see. Not much, but something. Somehow, from somewhere, light was getting into the tunnel.

After that, it got easier. Even Sadie helped. I'd

given her a sherbet lemon and she seemed to be over the worst of her panic attack. She was talking again, still not quite normal, but not in a total panic.

'It's starting to slope up,' she said. 'We're coming to the surface.'

We broke into a run, turning a corner, until we saw sunlight streaming in through a hole at the end of the tunnel. There was the myrtle bush, bright, brilliant green in the morning sun.

Myrt's head was poking through the bush, tongue lolling, like she was having the time of her life.

We burst through into blinding daylight and the smell of the leaves shook me back in time, or maybe

forward, to a memory.

All of sudden, all I wanted to do was cry.

I sobbed, still on my knees. Sadie hugged me, which was weird, but I didn't care. We'd solved the Riddle of the Sphinx's Butt; we were going to find my mum. Everything was going to be all right. Mum would solve everything; she'd rescue Johnnie from the volcano; she'd fix Dad, fix the time machine, everything. Mum's a fixer.

I knew it.

But if I'd known then what was going to happen next I'd have saved some tears for later.

You see, I thought I'd seen the worst thing ever when I opened that freezer and found Dad.

But I hadn't.

HOW TO SURVIVE THE WORST THING EVER

It took whole minutes for our eyes to get back to being able to see in the bright sunshine.

We were still in the desert; that was obvious. But who knew how far we'd gone, creeping along through the night? The tunnel had come up inside a steep, narrow valley, and we were right at the bottom, with huge cliffs on either side.

I chased after Myrt as she dashed about, but I needn't have bothered, because it was tiny. There was no way out, and no way in; the little gorge was the perfect hiding place. Sheer stone walls on each side gave shade to fruit trees next to a stream: plums, apricots, figs, and even an apple tree. We were in a little oasis, sealed off from the desert by unclimbable walls.

Myrt had found an opening on the far side, a cave in the wall of rock. Some vegetables were growing in a little patch outside it, and a channel had been dug in the ground so water could be sent from the stream.

I watched Myrt and listened to the tinkle as the stream ran over rocks and I smelled the green of a garden. Our very own Garden of Eden.

Sadie was acting a bit weird, lying on the ground and making angels in the dirt. Then she sat up and looked at me.

'Thank you,' she said, and then lay back down.

That's when Myrt started barking. She was still outside the little cave, but now she turned to look at me.

'Come on,' that bark said. Then she disappeared

inside, and I knew that I had to follow.

There was only one person on Earth who could turn this barren little gorge into the Garden of Eden.

My mum.

HOW TO MEET YOUR MUM

The cave was bigger on the inside than it looked on the outside.

'Mum?' I said loudly, and my voice echoed back at me.

You'd think my eyes would go back quickly into night mode, but they didn't. I tripped over a little wooden stool, and then I heard a voice:

'I knew you'd come.'

There was some fumbling and I saw a spark as an oil lamp flickered into life.

There was a kind of bed, with an old lady lying in it. Myrt was wagging her whole body in excitement, but the old lady slumped back, exhausted by her efforts with the lamp. I stepped a bit closer.

The lady looked a bit like Gran, except even older. Her skin was thin, like school toilet paper. Her eyes were glazy and white, and I suddenly realized she couldn't see me. Not properly. Maybe not at all.

'I knew you'd come,' she said again.

Her voice was old and scratchy, but it was unmistakable now. I felt my face start to burn and I reached out. But then I saw her hands for the first time. They were blue, nobbled with veins, and they looked painful, even to touch. I pulled back.

'Mum?'

But I didn't need an answer. I knew. This was Mum.

But it wasn't Mum. It wasn't *my* mum. My mum was full of life. This was Mum with everything sucked away.

I wanted to cry but couldn't. Some things are too awful for tears.

'Is that really you, Mum?'

The old woman smiled. She had no teeth and I was close enough to smell her now. She was rotting away.

'I knew you'd come,' she said again, smiling as she shut her eyes. I was glad not to look at them.

'You're a bit late, you know,' she said, eyes still shut. 'It's been sixty years.'

'But we came right away.' That was a stupid thing to say and I corrected myself. 'We followed your instructions. Dad's instructions. On the shoe.'

As I said it, I took off Johnnie's rucksack and yanked out the shoe.

'Look,' I said, pointing at it. 'It says 5000 BCE.'

And then I looked closer.

E&J, help! We're stuck in 5000 BCE, 29.9753° N, 31.1376° E

50o0 BCE.

That number had always looked a bit odd, and now I looked again, you could see where part of it had been scratched away. Like the top of a six had been scratched off to make it look like a zero.

It wasn't 5000 BCE, it was 5060 BCE!

Was it just dumb luck? Or had someone scratched it away on purpose?

'How long have you been here on your own, Mum?' I asked. But I already knew the answer to that too. Dad must have been frozen for sixty years. She must have spent sixty years here, all alone. Working her little garden, growing food, eating, sleeping, waking, waiting . . . all alone.

She seemed to nod off at that point, only to speak up a second later.

'I've stopped him every time, you know.'

'Stopped him doing what?'

'Blowing the top off that pyramid. But he just keeps trying. You're here now. Johnnie'll think of something clever.'

She started coughing. A hacking cough that seemed to rattle her entire body. It was a few minutes before she was able to speak again.

'Your dad always called you the Girl Who Never Gives Up. Do you know why he called you that?' She reached out and I touched her for the first time. She felt cold.

And then I heard Sadie's voice behind me.

'OMG, look at that,' she said.

I ran out of the cave.

I didn't stop until I reached the stream. I sank my head into the water to freeze my brain.

I just knelt there, wanting everything to go numb.

But there's only so long you can stick your head underwater.

I came up, dripping and shivering. Sadie Snickpick was just staring at me.

'So what are we gonna do now?' she asked.

I wanted to scream at her, but all the energy had gone out of me. Instead, a river of quiet words came pouring out.

'How should I know? Don't you get it? We're sixty years too late. We've blown it. It's over. Everything's gone. Dad's gone, Mum's about to die and Johnnie's about to be sacrificed in a supervolcano. And that's not even the worst of it. Noah's going to blow so much ash into the sky that the whole human race is going to be wiped out before we've even been born.'

'It's not that bad. We just need to work together,'

said Sadie, frowning. She was starting to look like her old angry self again.

'Yes. It really is that bad.'

'So what, we should just stay here for ninety years and give up and grow old like your horrible old mum?'

Horrible old mum.

Sadie's words exploded in my head and I grabbed her. Grabbed her hair and pulled. Sadie's face filled up with fear, and that's happened, like, never. She even cried out when I pulled her head towards me.

'What do you want me to say, Sadie? That I've got a brilliant plan that's going to save the entire planet?'

Then I heard a cry from the cave.

It was Mum.

She was calling for me.

She was close to dying and she was calling for me.

And just when I thought things couldn't get any worse, I heard something else.

I heard drums, from across the desert.

The same dread pattern as before.

DUM, dum-dum-dum.

DUM, dum-dum-dum.

It was exactly the same beat, a drumbeat that could mean only one thing.

Human sacrifice.

And I knew with a sudden, heart-crushing horror that my little baby brother was about to be burned alive.

It was like I was being torn in two. I just stood there, frozen in indecision.

Dad always says, 'Life is the choices you make,' but in that moment I knew that, whatever I did, I had to say goodbye to Mum first.

And so I chose.

I chose to go back into the cave.

HOW TO SAY GOODBYE TO YOUR MUM

Ten-year-olds are never supposed to see their parents die. But then they're not supposed to see them grow old either, or be frozen in carbonite. They're not supposed to travel back, to a time before they're even born, and save the world from maniacs.

Mum was exactly as I'd left her: eyes shut; lips, face, everything grey. For a horrible moment, I thought she was already dead. But then I saw her breathing.

'I love you, Mum.'

I don't know if she heard me, but that wasn't important somehow. I squeezed her hand three times; that seemed important. She'd taught it to me on my first day of school, just as we got to the gate.

Three squeezes meant, 'I love you.'

And then she squeezed back.

But only twice.

Tears ran down my face and I said, 'I have to go, Mum. I have to save Johnnie.'

And then she gave my hand a third squeeze and I let out a sob.

'I'm sorry, Mum. But I have to go.'

'Don't worry,' she said, her voice impossibly quiet. 'I can wait a bit longer. Just come back earlier next time. Go rescue your little brother, sweetie.'

I knew, as her chin flopped back down, that I would come back. No matter how impossible, I'd come back and save her. I'd never give up.

But first I had to save Johnnie. He was about to be burned alive. And, if Mum had been able to, she'd have yelled at me to save her little Johnnie. And that's what my brain screamed too.

HOW TO RESCUE YOUR BROTHER FROM BEING BURNED ALIVE

I ran out of the cave and didn't stop. Back to the myrtle bush, through the crack in the rock and down into the musty passageway. I didn't look back, but I didn't have to. I knew Myrt would be with me. Sadie followed too.

'Go on, Myrty, find Johnnie.'

This time Myrt didn't run off. Brilliant dog. She kept scampering back and forth to make sure we were keeping up. It was like she knew we had to get back to save Johnnie. And the miracle of Myrt was that she'd got the whole labyrinth mapped out with her nose. We sped through the passages, mile after mile, following that brilliant, brilliant dog.

We couldn't hear the drums underground, not really. But I could hear them banging in my head, and I could see Johnnie's worried little potato face too.

We ran on and on. Even Sadie struggled to keep up, but fear made me fast because, all the while we ran, I could hear my own heart drumming that terrible drumbeat in my ears.

Despite our speed, it must have taken an hour to get back to the Sphinx. An hour to do the journey that had taken us five hours the night before. Myrt, bless her, didn't make a single wrong turn.

I only slowed when the passage started to rise. We were nearing the end, and I hesitated before entering the final chamber, the freezer chamber. It suddenly felt like a lifetime ago, opening that fridge door and finding Dad. But, as I peered carefully into the chamber, my heart stopped. The Mysterious Sarcophagus #2 was gone. And so was the python.

Whatever that meant, it was bad.

I heard drums again, but not just in my head: drums for real. It was the same steady pattern as before, and that had to be good. We still had time to save Johnnie.

'What now?' said Sadie in a harsh whisper.

I ignored her; it still didn't feel right, Sadie asking me to make all the decisions. I climbed up the uneven stone stairs and back into the light.

Just in time to witness the Greatest Human Sacrifice of All Time.

Or maybe even stop it.

HOW TO STOP THE GREATEST HUMAN SACRIFICE OF ALL TIME

The sky was a solid chunk of blue, with the desert shining white beneath it. The dunes seemed bigger somehow, including the sand-covered pyramid that was the biggest of them all.

It was dotted with people, all near the top. Some had drums, some didn't, and right at the top, standing astride our new sofa, stood the Boy Noah. He had a stick, or a spear, and was shouting over the noise of the drums.

Next to the sofa was a sarcophagus. It didn't take a genius to guess which one.[39]

---

39 Sarcophagus #2 obviously. I'm pretty sure that in the history of the world no one has ever sacrificed ice cream. Ever.

And then I saw Johnnie. Impossibly small, wobbling on the arm of the sofa, and looking down into the pyramid. They hadn't even bothered to tie him up. How could I have left him?

I couldn't hear what Noah was shouting, but I

didn't need to. The drums told me everything. They were getting faster, and Johnnie was being spear-prodded off the sofa and into the pyramid.

Any thought of a plan evaporated and I just ran towards them, screaming at the top of my voice.

Running uphill through the sand was like running in a bad dream. My legs were pumping, but my feet just seemed to slip and slide. No one could hear me. I shouted and screamed, but no one heard. Johnnie was right at the edge of the sofa now – he had nowhere else to go but down.

I opened my mouth, but I couldn't scream any louder.

Then, from behind me, came a whistle.

One of those PE teacher, thumb-and-finger whistles that stops you dead in your tracks. It was Sadie.

She whistled again, this time even louder.

And the drums stopped.

The drums stopped, and all eyes turned to me, red-faced and panting halfway up the hill. Johnnie inched back from the edge of the sofa and I felt a surge of relief.

Noah shouted, and soon there were dozens of Stone Agers streaming down the dune towards us. This wasn't exactly a rescue, but somehow that didn't matter. What mattered was Johnnie. And whatever happened to us now we'd face it together.

HOW TO FACE IT TOGETHER

It wasn't long before we joined Johnnie on the sofa. There were spears everywhere now; *everyone* seemed to have one. Noah tipped back his animal mask so we could see the sneer on his face, and called one of his minions to tie Sadie's hands behind her back.[40]

If we'd saved Johnnie's life, we hadn't saved very much of it. But he looked so pleased to see us, hugging Myrt and smiling at me as though I was about to sort everything out.

The spears jabbed us further on to the sofa, and I looked down into the guts of the pyramid for the

---

40 He didn't bother tying me up. He clearly saw both me and Johnst as a couple of useless wimps.

first time. That's when I fully realized just how doomed we all were.

The great smelting pots from before were all gone, and the children too. In their place was just a well of black powder. A great mass of gunpowder that filled the pyramid and only needed one spark to obliterate the world.

You had to take your hat off to Noah. Even as a skinny ten-year-old, he was a really effective completer-finisher.

I looked at Sadie, but she was too busy wrestling with the rope round her wrists to notice. This was no longer our sofa; it was a Frying Pan of Death. And the fire was about to be lit.

Noah shook a box of matches to get my attention.

'You never stop with the surprises, do you, Eliza Lemon? I see you escaped the labyrinth of death.[41]

---

41 At least that's cleared that up.

THE FRYING PAN OF DEATH

How'd you do it?'

He looked genuinely curious, but I was determined not to give him the satisfaction of knowing we'd used Myrt's genius nose.

'I guess you'll never find out, will you?' I said, quietly pleased by the look on his face.

And then Myrt barked, and his scowl turned to a smile.

'The dog, of course! What an idiot. I shoulda thoughta that.' Noah fiddled with the tip of his spear as he spoke; it looked sharp. 'And did you find ya momma? Or is she dead by now?'

I turned to Johnnie, and his little face collapsed.

'Johnst, she's still alive. We just have to get the time machine working and go back to the right time.'

'What do you mean the right time?'

'We're not supposed to be here, Johnnie, not now. We need to go back another sixty years.' As I said it, and saw the look of horror on Johnnie's face, I suddenly knew what had happened to the message on Dad's shoe.

'It was you, wasn't it?' I said, turning to Noah, 'You changed the date in Dad's message.'

Noah nodded.

'And you planted the tree. In our garden? This

was all a trap, wasn't it? This was always just a stupid trap.'

Noah never stopped smiling.

'I genuinely did need your time machine. Mine really did get bashed up. When I made the jump from 5060 BCE to 5000 BCE.' He looked around at the Stone Agers. 'I needed those extra sixty years to give my Parrot Poo Cult enough time to collect the poo for the bomb.'

I thought back to Johnnie's calculations in my journal. In sixty years, they could collect enough parrot poo for half a nuclear bomb's worth of gunpowder.

I turned to Johnnie. 'It was a trap, Johnst. He changed the year on the shoe. We need to go back to 5060 BCE. That's when Mum and Dad landed.'

Johnnie looked confused. 'But how?'

'That was the easy bit.' Noah seemed to be

enjoying this. 'I caught your dad with that shoe sixty years ago. It was the perfect thing; I just had to change the six to a zero and 5060 BCE became 5000 BCE.'

'But how did it get in the tree?' Sadie finally had a question.

Noah smiled. 'What are worshippers for? I sent twelve disciples to your garden. They planted the tree, they tended it, and over the years the tree grew round it, locking the shoe inside. From father to son and mother to daughter, they passed down the secret of the tree. I'm guessing, of course – I only sent them last Tuesday. But, by the time you were born, they must have been guarding that shoe for millennia. Imagine that – seven thousand years, generation after generation, always believing . . . believing in me. Their one true god!'

As he shouted, Noah raised his spear and a

hundred voices cried out as one. It was creepy, I tell you. They really were a cult, and he was their leader. I gulped, actually gulped, and looked at Johnnie, then Sadie. We were well and truly stuffed.

Noah pointed his spear at my face. 'This ends now – the human race ends now – and for ever. And no meddling kids with a time machine are gonna stop me.'

He held his hand up high and the drums began to beat once more. As I looked at Sadie, then Johnnie, and finally Myrt, I realized I didn't have the first clue how we'd get out of the frying pan without ending up in the fire.

HOW TO GET OUT OF A FRYING PAN WITHOUT ENDING UP IN THE FIRE

You'd think one of us could have come up with some sort of a plan. But when you're balanced on a time-machine sofa, hanging over half-a-nuclear-bomb's-worth of gunpowder that's about to catch fire and destroy the whole human race for ever . . . and the only way off is through a hedge of spears . . . and there are really loud drums playing . . .

Well, you get the point.

With all that going on, any plan is a big ask. Even a rubbish one.

'This is how it's gonna work,' Noah shouted over

the boom of the drums. 'You're going down there –'
he pointed into the pyramid with his spear – 'while
I go onwards and upwards . . . to the *future.*'

He pulled a controller out of his pocket. It wasn't
small and black like ours – it glistened bright in the
sunlight, all the colours of the rainbow.

'See, you idiot,' I heard Sadie say to Johnnie
behind my back. She was still struggling against the
ropes around her wrists. 'Make it big and rainbow-y
next time so we can't lose it.'

I turned to Johnst. He looked so sad.

I wanted to say something. I wanted to tell
him everything would be all right, like Dad would
have done. But then I saw the sarcophagus and
remembered Dad might never say anything ever
again. And my throat shut tight.

Noah's plan was perfect. My family were the
only people in the history of the world who could go

back in time to stop him, and he'd made absolutely, totally and completely sure none of us were getting out of here alive.

The Stone Agers gripped their spears and beat their drums with zeal. They were about to learn about blind faith the hard way, as they sent their stupid leader triumphantly back to the future, and killed the rest of us in the process.

A future without humans.

A future he could build afresh.

I looked desperately about, but the more I tried to

think, the more hopeless everything seemed.

My face must have looked awful, because Johnnie reached out and squeezed my hand three times.

'Thanks for coming back for me,' he said, leaving behind a sticky sweet. 'It's my last one.'

I looked down at the sherbet lemon, and then I looked at Johnst.

'It's all right, Johnnie,' I said. 'You have it.'

Tears were running down his cheeks as he put it in his mouth, and I squeezed his arm.

'Sherbet lemons always make everything better, remember.'

The drums beat faster.

'Are you ready for one last game of lava floor, Eliza Lemon?' Noah shouted over the noise. Then his spear jabbed forward, and suddenly I was tipping backwards.

As I began to fall, I remember thinking, *Shouldn't*

I start panicking round about now?

But I didn't. Because just then, Johnnie began to cough.

He'd hit the fizzy bit in his sherbet lemon.

SADIE SNICKPICK
IS A BULLY

JOHNNIE IS CHOKING
ON A SHERBET LEMON

HOW TO WIN A GAME
OF LAVA FLOOR

So here we are again. It's 5000 BCE and
I'm falling off a sofa, into a artificial
volcano that's about to explode and
wipe the entire human race off the
of the planet.

THAT'S ME, I'M THE HERO
OF THIS STORY, AND I'M
NOT PANICKING.

ARTIFICIAL VOLCANO
THAT'S ABOUT TO BLOW

Johnnie coughed up his sweet and it flew in a big arc, landing on Sadie's shoe. It just sat there, stuck with spit. And then Sadie flicked her foot and the sweet flew again, except this time it shot Noah right in the eye, like a bullet.

I toppled back in slow motion, but I didn't even flap my arms. My brain was too busy. Because that teamwork with the sherbet lemon had shown me something I needed to see.

Johnnie was right: I was just a drip. One little drip in a mighty ocean. I couldn't do this alone, but I didn't have to. We'd all played our part: Johnnie made the time machine, Myrt helped in the maze, even Sadie had saved my life. Twice.

As if to prove my point, Myrt leapt forward and bit Noah on the leg. And Johnnie, bless him, grabbed the other leg.

As I fell backwards, I knew what to do.

I didn't have to save everyone, I just had to do my bit.

My little bit.

I grabbed the end of Noah's spear. The sharp end.

The flint cut into my hand, but I didn't care. I held on to it and watched Noah's face as he lost his balance and came toppling down after me.

And together we fell into the volcano.

HOW TO FALL INTO
A VOLCANO

Except it wasn't both of us. It was all of us. Well, not Sadie, but Johnnie and Myrt were too stupid to let go of Noah. The four of us fell and I screamed in frustration. We landed with a crunch and a cloud of black dust, and all the air was knocked out of me.

The powder was so powdery, I immediately started to sink. I hadn't thought of that. I flapped about, struggling to stay afloat, desperate to find Johnnie and Myrt. Until I found Johnnie's chubby arm and gripped it.

He shouted in pain, but I didn't care.

'Johnnie, get out.'

His face looked at me as if to say, 'Are you crazy?'

Noah was quite literally swimming through gunpowder towards us. Myrt was sinking and there was nothing I could do to save her. But I could save my brother.

'Johnnie, now!' I shouted, dragging him towards me. I somehow got under his feet and pushed him up the side as he struggled to pull himself on to the edge. The more I pushed, the deeper I sank, but with one great heave my head went under and Johnnie was launched to safety.

It was awful under there. Like black quicksand that fills your ears and nose and mouth. If you ever get sucked into quicksand, never scream. It just makes it worse.

Somehow, I don't know how, I got my head back above the powder. I opened my eyes and immediately saw Myrt. She was trying to swim to me, but Noah had her by the tail, and her wild eyes told me he was winning. Then I saw why he'd grabbed her. Because in her mouth, in all the colours of the rainbow, was the controller.[42]

I grabbed it, and Noah let out a howl. Still struggling not to sink, I lifted it high above the surface and aimed it at the sofa.

'It's over, Noah. You failed,' I said, shaking the controller so he could see it. 'There's nothing you can do.'

He looked at me and blinked, slowly.

'There is one thing, Eliza Lemon,' he said coldly, and lifted up a box of matches. My eyes must have grown huge, because he laughed at the look on my face. And then, without another word, he took out a match.

He wasn't bluffing. He was going to end

---

42 It's worth mentioning that, up until this point, Myrt had never retrieved anything in her life.

everything, even himself.

I frantically dialled the controller to the Year 2053, but, hands above his head, Noah struck a match against the side of the box.

This is the end, I thought.

But then the match went out.

HOW TO SURVIVE THE END

I'm quite proud that my next thought was about Johnnie. I looked up and saw he'd landed on the wrong side of the pyramid.

Trust Johnnie.

'Johnnie, get back on the sofa.'

'But what about you?'

'Just get on the sofa!'

'I can't.'

'What do you mean?'

Noah was scrabbling for another match. I pushed my body up out of the gunpowder, desperate to see better. And then I saw – the sarcophagus with Dad in it was blocking Johnnie's way.

'Just jump, Johnnie.'

He had to jump across the corner – it was only a metre.

'I can't, 'Liza. My leg.'

I heard Noah fumbling with the second match.

'Yes, you can, Johnnie. You're stronger than you think.'

'Just jump!' shouted Sadie. She'd finally got her hands free. 'I'll catch you!'

I looked into Johnnie's face for one last time.

'Johnnie, you have to jump. You're the only one who can go back and save Mum. Sadie will look after you. She'll help you.'

But would she?

And then I saw him jump.

It was feeble, even for a five-year-old. He leapt like a stiff old man, and he just seemed to hang there in mid-air.

Then Sadie's arm flung out, and with a single

hand she grabbed him by the back of his T-shirt. For an awful moment, I thought he'd slip right out of it, but Sadie was already pulling him in, like he weighed nothing.

Noah was smiling, the second match was lit, and I saw him let go.

The match fell.

We were out of time.

I pressed the volume button on the rainbow controller and imagined the blue lattice of light growing bigger and bigger. Scanning through Johnnie, through the sofa. I kept pressing the button over and over. Imagining it scanning through Dad, frozen in his sarcophagus. I imagined a lot in that frozen moment. Sadie making breakfast while Johnnie defrosted Dad. Imagined them going back to save Mum. But, all the while, I watched the flame of Noah's match as it hit the black powder and fizzed with life.

I stopped kicking my legs and started sinking. Myrt was going under too, just a little nose poking above the powder.

I looked up to see Johnnie still struggling on to the sofa. His legs dangling over the side, kicking about as he struggled to climb on. Sadie Snickpick was reaching over, and for a horrible moment I thought she was about to push him off, but she pulled, yanking him up by his shorts. A wedgie to save his life.

I went under a third time, Sadie's face looking down at me, and, despite the sneer that never leaves her lips and the catty eyes that always look ready to scratch, I smiled at her. She was Johnnie's only hope, and she was saving him.

Sometimes in life you just have to trust people. They may let you down, or tell everyone your secrets, they might even pick a new BFF and leave you feeling like a total loser. It doesn't matter. That's their problem, not yours. And, in that moment, I trusted Sadie Snickpick. Trusted her to look after my little brother when his mum and dad and big sister couldn't. When he didn't even have his Myrty to keep him safe.

Sadie pulled, and Johnnie's wriggling little legs disappeared on to the sofa.

'Bye, Johnnie,' I said, but I couldn't see him.

The sofa, the sarcophagus, even the side of the pyramid, everything was disappearing, like it was being rubbed out by giant eraser. The time machine was working.

Then noise, as the gunpowder flared into a shuddering blast that shook everything.

Just imagine what it's like right in the middle of a nuclear explosion. Well, it was like that, but about half as bad. Which is still pretty, incredibly, deathly bad.

Except, even as it exploded, the flames were being rubbed out too. The time machine was obliterating everything around it.

I took one last look at Noah's angry, screaming face, and then he disappeared too.

Then it was my turn. And for the second time that week I was obliterated.

SOME TIME LATER

Now, you may be wondering how anyone writes the sentence: 'And for the second time that week I was obliterated.'

It's what Johnnie likes to call 'a paradox'.

And, believe me, I completely understand how annoying a paradox can be. And this one makes about as much sense as:

MY GRAN WHEN SHE SAYS:

SOMETIMES YOU HAVE TO BE CRUEL TO BE KIND!

Stupid Paradox!

OR . . .

MY DAD WHEN HE SAYS:

JUST DO AS I SAY, NOT AS I DO.

OR. . .

Stupid Paradox!

Stupid Paradox!

OF COURSE I KNOW YOU CAN DO IT. IT'S JUST THAT I THOUGHT YOU MIGHT NEED SOME HELP!

Well, you're gonna have to forgive me, but I can't explain it either.

You see, the next thing I knew was that Myrt was licking my face. I opened my eyes and pushed her away and found myself in this weird room. It's white and square, like I'm in a light box. The floor's soft enough to sleep on, and I've got all my stuff. Well, all the stuff in Johnnie's rucksack, including this journal and the stubby pencil I'm writing this with. And Myrt's here too. I think I mentioned that.

I've tried to get out, obviously, but there's not even a door. It's like I died and I'm trapped in heaven. Or maybe hell. Except Myrt's here too, so it can't be hell.

But that's not even the weirdest thing. The weirdest thing is that a few minutes ago the wall disappeared and someone put a plate of pesto pasta and a glass of guava juice on the floor next to me. And there was a letter. From Johnnie.

Even that's not the weirdest-weirdest thing.

The weirdest-weirdest thing is that the man who brought the food looked exactly like my PE teacher, Mr Murray. Remember him?

The one who's spent the last five years trying to kill me.

EDITOR'S NOTE

When this journal arrived on my desk, I assumed it was a prank. No one's seen Eliza Lemon since she disappeared nine months ago. The internet is full of conspiracy theories and 'Lemon sightings' and 'Lemon hunts'.

I'm pretty sure Eliza Lemon would get in touch if she could, if only because we owe her several million pounds in book royalties. So you can see why I thought this manuscript was a bad joke. But then I read it and it just has to be genuine. The handwriting is hers, for one thing, and there was even the letter from Johnnie tucked in the back.

Eliza, if you ever read this note, please contact us. Let us know you're safe.

Wibbly Cottage,

Lower Biscuit

4th Sept 2053

Hi Eliza,

I hope you're OK. So, good news about saving the
world. I'm back home and it's just like we left it.
Which is a bit of a mess, to be honest.

It's weird being on my own. Dad's here, obviously,
but I haven't managed to defrost him yet. It all
looks a LOT more complicated than we thought.
I'm sure he'll be all right, but I just want to make
absolutely sure I'm doing it right and there's not
much on the internet about how to defrost your
frozen dad.

It's my first day at school tomorrow and I don't
want to go. But if I don't go then they'll send
someone round to the house and figure out that

Dad's frozen and everything. I'm trying to get the sofa fixed so I can go and rescue Mum like you said, but it's pretty bashed up. I don't know if I can do it without you. I don't know if I can do anything without you, 'Liza. Why can't you just come back?

You said Sadie would look after me, but she just went off on her bike as soon as we got here. And now I don't know what to do. I'm scared. Why can't you just come home? I know you survived the volcano – I saw you and Myrt being scanned. How did you do that BTW? You must have hit the volume button A LOT because it scanned a ton of gunpowder as well. Most of it's still on the lawn, but I don't know where you and Myrt went, or when you went, or why you didn't just come back here.

Anyhow, I've figured out how to copy this letter using what's left of the time machine and I'm going to copy it a zillion times and send it to every year all the way out to the Year 3000. If you get it, please write back; there's loads of things I'm not sure about. Like where you get school uniform from and where you go after you get to the school gates and how do you order lunch?

Lots of love, Eliza, and see you soon,

Johnnie

x x x x x

x

x

x x x

Secret 55: How to Lie

Do	Don't
Look at their whole face	Look into their eyeballs
breathe	breathe too much
talk	talk too much
swallow	swallow too hard
smile	smile too much

!#CHEAT CODE#!

Still can't do it? then use this genius Cheat Code: Sing 'Happy Birthday' in your head while you're lying. You'll sound and look a bit distracted and **_no one_** looks distracted when they're lying.

ACKNOWLEDGEMENTS

It takes a village to raise a book. As I slap the keyboard with my fists I do so in the sure knowledge that Lowri Ribbons and Ali Dougal will edit it into brilliance, that Katie Abey will perform illustrative wonders, and the whole team at Simon & Schuster will create the marvel that is this book. The text designer Jo Garden has worked miracles, Leena Lane and Jane Tait have copy-edited and proofread with bewildering meticulosity, and Jesse Green and Sean Williams have produced a cover so good it deserves an award. Thank you, all.

THE ADVENTURE CONTINUES IN:

HOW TO SURVIVE THE FUTURE

COMING IN 2023

LOOK OUT FOR ELIZA AND JOHNNIE'S FIRST ADVENTURE - AVAILABLE NOW!

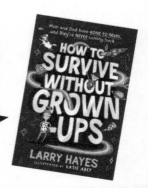